this is where it ends

MARIEKE NIJKAMP

sourcebooks
fire

Published by Sourcebooks Fire, an imprint of Sourcebooks, Inc.
P.O. Box 4410, Naperville, Illinois 60567-4410
(630) 961-3900
Fax: (630) 961-2168
sourcebooks.com

Library of Congress Cataloging-in-Publication Data

Nijkamp, Marieke.
 This is where it ends / Marieke Nijkamp.
    pages cm
 Summary: Minutes after the principal of Opportunity High School in Alabama
finishes her speech welcoming the student body to a new semester, they discover that
the auditorium doors will not open and someone starts shooting as four teens, each
with a personal reason to fear the shooter, tell the tale from separate perspectives.
 (alk. paper)
 [1. School shootings--Fiction. 2. High schools--Fiction. 3. Schools--Fiction. 4.
Interpersonal relations--Fiction.] I. Title.
 PZ7.1.N55Thi 2016
 [Fic]--dc23
                        2015016026

Printed and bound in the United States of America.
LSC 10 9 8 7 6 5 4 3 2 1

To my mom, with love.

CHAPTER ONE

CLAIRE

The starter gun shatters the silence, releasing the runners from their blocks.

Track season starts in a couple weeks, but no one has told Coach Lindt about winter. He's convinced that the only way to get us into shape is to practice—even when my breath freezes right in front of me.

This is Opportunity, Alabama. Sane people don't leave their homes when it's white and frosty outside. We stock up on canned food, drink hot chocolate until we succumb to sugar comas, and pray to be saved from the cold.

Still, Coach Lindt's start-of-season training beats Principal Trenton's long and arduous start-of-semester speech—virtue, hard work, and the proper behavior of young ladies and gentlemen. After almost four years at Opportunity High, I can recite her words from memory, which is exactly what I did for Matt at breakfast this morning—responsibility, opportunity ("no pun intended"), and her favorite, our school motto: *We Shape the Future*.

It sounds glorious, but with months left until graduation, I have no clue what the future looks like. If Opportunity shaped me, I didn't notice. Running, I know. This track, I know. One step after another after another. It doesn't matter what comes next as long as I keep moving forward.

My foot slips, and I stumble.

From his position on the field, Coach curses. "Claire, attention! One misstep's the difference between success and failure."

Straightening, I refocus.

A familiar laugh colors the still morning. "Did you freeze up over holiday break, Sarge? A snail could catch up with you floundering like that." On the straightaway of the track, Chris falls into step with me.

I suck in a breath before I answer him. "Oh, shut up."

My best friend only laughs louder. The even rhythm of his footsteps and his breathing challenge me to find my pace. His presence steadies me like it always does. At six-foot-five and with sun-touched hair and blue eyes, Chris is not just our best runner but also Opportunity's poster-boy athlete. On uniform days, the freshman girls fawn over him.

With Chris by my side, my stride shortens. The other two runners on our varsity team are far behind us, on the other side of the field. Chris and I move in perfect synchrony, and the very air parts before us.

Nothing can touch us. Not snow. Not even time.

....

TOMÁS

Time's up. The small clock on the bookshelf strikes ten with an annoying little tune, and I thumb through the tabs in front of me at supersonic speed. *C'mon, c'mon, c'mon.*

It only took superglue—strategically squirted on the desk drawers of my favorite Spanish teacher, Mr. Look-At-Me-Strutting-My-Stuff-Like-A-Walking-Midlife-Crisis—for Far and me to find our way to the administrative office. But it took both our student IDs before we managed to jiggle the lock on Principal Trenton's door. And it'll all be for nothing if I can't find the file I'm looking for. I scan the folders in the filing cabinet. When an elbow pokes my side, I startle. "Dammit, Far. What the hell?"

Fareed rolls his eyes and gestures for me to keep quiet. *Someone's in the hallway*, he mouths. He tiptoes back to the door.

Crap.

How do I explain this? "No, ma'am, I'm not doing anything, just breaking into school records"?

Whatever. I'm sure I have a legal right to see my own

3

permanent record, so I can always use that as my excuse. The fact that these folders just *happened* to be "Last Names, A–C" instead of "Last Names, M–N" is nothing more than a coincidence. No one knows whose file I'm looking for, except Far. And even he doesn't know the whole reason.

If anything, I can always "find" Al-Sahar, Fareed as a cover. The school administration can't even file his name right.

Still.

A door opens and closes. A lock clicks.

Footsteps squeak on the linoleum outside the administrative office.

Footsteps that pause before the principal's door—our door.

I quietly push the file drawer shut. Better not to stir up trouble—*more* trouble—if I get caught red-handed.

Far and I both hold our breath.

After what feels like forever, the footsteps move on. Whomever it was, they're not out to get us. Not today.

....

AUTUMN

"…it's all a matter of the decisions you make, today and every day. Your behavior reflects not only on yourself but also on your parents, your family, and your school.

4

"Here at Opportunity, we pride ourselves on shaping the doctors, lawyers, and politicians of tomorrow. And it's the choices you make now that will determine your future. You have to ask yourself how you can become the best you can be. Ask not what your school can do for you but what *you* can do for you."

Trenton holds the microphone loosely while she scans the crowd, as if memorizing every single face. So many students come and go, leaving nothing but the faintest impression, names scratched into desks and graffitied onto bathroom stalls, yet she knows us all.

All our hopes. All our heartbreaks. All our sleepless nights.

Her eyes linger on me, and my neck burns. I reach for the chair to my right, but it remains as it was when the assembly started. Empty.

To my left, Sylv groans. "After all these years, you'd think she'd come up with something more original."

"Don't you want to be the best you can be?" The words come out harsher than I intend.

She grumbles.

In truth, Sylv will have plenty of colleges to choose from. She's a shoo-in for all her dream schools. And I should be happy for her. I *am* happy for her.

But for me, college is the only way out of this misery, and Dad sure as hell isn't going to pay my ride. Not to study dance. "Look what happened to your mother," he'd say, as if I haven't counted the days, hours, minutes since Mom's accident. "Dance took everything from her. No daughter of mine is going into that business. Not if I can stop it."

So he tries to stop me—every day. And with Mom gone, there's no one to stop him. Not from drinking. Not from hitting me. There's no one to keep our family from falling apart.

I grip my crumpled coffee cup, grab the threadbare denim messenger bag from under my seat, and block out Ty's voice in the back of my mind. My brother would tell me that Principal Trenton's words are truer than I think, that the world is at my fingertips and it's up to me to make my future the best it can be.

I tried that and I lost. Now I'd rather escape.

....

SYLV

I sink deep into my seat and glance at the empty place next to Autumn. He's not coming after all. He'd have been here by now. He won't come. I'm safe here.

He won't come.

The knot in my stomach unfurls and recoils with every twist and turn of my mind. I could ask Autumn about

Tyler, but she's lost in memories. Today is two years since the accident. She refuses to share her grief with me—or anyone. Even when she smiles, she isn't the girl she used to be.

And I miss her.

Some days, when she thinks no one is watching, she still moves across the floor as if she's flying. *La golondrina*, Mamá used to call her. The swallow. All grace and beauty. When Autumn dances, all her worry falls away and she shines.

I wish she could dance forever.

Madre de Dios, how I wish I could watch her dance forever.

Instead, it is another Monday. Life goes on. The assembly is over, and Autumn holds herself ramrod straight. I'm the only one who knows she'll fly out of this cage and leave us all behind as soon as she can.

Meanwhile, next period is the last review for my AP U.S. History midterm, and I haven't even touched my books. Mamá had another one of her bad spells over break. We were supposed to go into town together last Saturday, but when Abuelo brought the car around, she barely recognized him. She didn't want to leave the house. She didn't understand where we were going. I sat with her for hours, talked to her—*listen, Mamá*—told her the stories that wove our family around her. She was disoriented for days afterward, and I can't shake the feeling that with every day that passes, she slips away like starlight at dawn.

At least history suits me. You already know if those stories will end happily.

CJ Johnson
@CadetCJJ
Sleeeeeeeeepy #OHS
10:01 AM

Jay Eyck
@JEyck32
@CadetCJJ #snodaylikeasnowday
10:01 AM

CJ Johnson
@CadetCJJ
@JEyck32 Bailing on assembly to sleep?
>_> #morelikehungoverday
10:01 AM

CJ Johnson
@CadetCJJ
@Claire_Morgan Can I order one of the
freshmen to bring me coffee?
10:02 AM

CHAPTER TWO

TOMÁS

I reach for the bowl on top of the desk and pop a few mints into my mouth. Far peeks around the principal's door. When he gives the all clear, I open the filing cabinet again. I haven't lost much work. Just time.

Principal Trenton may still live in the pre-digital era, but she's like a cyborg. She always speaks until ten sharp, leaving five minutes for announcements before the bell. By the end of the assembly, everyone has to run to make it to class on time for third period. Well, in theory. The teachers and other personnel are in the auditorium too, and they don't run.

So everyone pushes to leave, then strolls, dawdles, sneaks out for a smoke and some air (the two aren't mutually exclusive, *thank you very much*). After all, even nicotine and tar smell better than what my sis once described as our "odor-torium," a unique blend of testosterone, sweat, and burned coffee.

But we're cutting it far too close. "I hate paperwork."

"Maybe you should stay on the farm then," Fareed drawls. "Honest work and hard labor don't require brains."

"You're hilarious." My fingers skim his file, and I pull it out of the drawer. "D'you want to see the letter of recommendation Mr. O'Brian wrote for your college applications?"

He holds out his hands, and I toss him the file. A few sheets flutter from the folder before Far catches it.

"Barbarian."

I snort. "Sorry. Not sorry."

"I look so young and innocent in this picture," Fareed muses, staring at his cover sheet. For most of our class, the picture used by the administration is three years old, taken when we enrolled as freshmen. In his case, however—

"That was taken last year!"

"How you've corrupted me. Without your brilliant ideas, I'd have been a straight-A student, never in trouble with the law, girls following me everywhere."

"Sure." I pull another folder out of the filing cabinet. "Keep telling yourself that."

Fareed makes another comment, but I'm not paying attention. A familiar picture stares at me from the cover sheet.

Bingo.

Browne, Tyler. Gelled blond hair, pale eyes, and an oh-so-familiar blank look. The one time his eyes weren't glossed over with contempt was when I slammed his head into a locker. My fingers itch to do it again.

Does the administration note criminal charges in student records? Probably not when the files are this easy to access. Definitely not when said student dropped out at the end of last year. Besides, I don't even know if he *has* a criminal record. According to his grades, he was a perfectly respectable C student. Three years at Opportunity and Tyler coasted through all his classes.

He only—spectacularly—failed Humanity 101.

The latest note in his file is unmistakable though: *Reenrolling. Effective immediately.*

Sylvia mentioned it this weekend. It was the first time she's confided in me in months. She looked ready to puke her guts out, she was so scared, but she refused to tell me why. So here I am, breaking into school records. To make sure she's safe. Twin-brother privileges.

Not that I'll ever admit to that or even hint that I care. Twin-brother reputation.

I lean against the principal's desk and read.

Date of birth, address—boring. Emergency contact information for father, mother deceased. Last school, date of admission—nothing I don't already know. Present class: not applicable. Not yet.

SAT score: 2140.

Huh. A closet genius.

Maybe that explains why, despite his bravado, Tyler never made good on any of his threats. He may be a maggot, but he's the smartest kind: a harmless one.

....

AUTUMN

My back aches. I roll my shoulders to loosen the knotted muscles. Sylv lingers instead of rejoining the rest of her class. She cracks her knuckles with sharp snaps. "Are you okay?"

"I…" I hesitate.

I woke up drenched in sweat last night, expecting a knock at the door like two years ago. But this morning was breakfast as usual. Ty was nowhere to be found, and after this weekend, I didn't mind. *Figures*. Dad didn't bother to get up. He started—or never stopped—drinking last night. These days, he doesn't even try to hide it. When Mom was still alive, he only drank when she was away and only during the darkest times. He still knew how to smile then, and he could make both Ty and me laugh.

Now he's angry at the entire world, at anything that reminds him of Mom.

At me.

I don't know how to put all that into words. *I'm not*

okay. I haven't been okay in a long time. It isn't just Mom's death. Dad—sometimes I'm afraid.

And Ty… *I'm afraid I'll lose Ty too.*

But Sylv and Ty hate each other. How can I begin to make her understand?

She places her hand on my arm, then remembers where we are and nervously tucks a long, black curl behind her ears. Her bright-blue top matches her eyeliner, which makes her eyes sparkle. At Opportunity, where so many of us prefer to stay hidden, she's the brightest spotlight on the darkest stage. She looks at me expectantly. "It's understandable, you know. Anniversaries can be difficult. You can be sad. No one will judge you, least of all me."

I nod, but the words still won't form. The voices ebb and flow around us as students climb the raked aisles between the four blocks of seating. Sylv's eyes flick to the other side of the auditorium, where some of the football players are getting loud.

I shrug. "It's fine. I'm fine."

She'd never understand. No one does.

I'm counting down the minutes to seventh period, when the music room behind the stage is dark and deserted. In the shadows, I'll be alone.

I'll be safe.

Sylv opens her mouth, but before she can say anything, a girl from her class appears at her elbow—Asha, I think.

She used to get into arguments with my brother before he dropped out. I can't—I don't want to keep up with all of them. They will only bind me to this place, and it hurts so much to care.

Asha clings to her AP U.S. History textbook. Under strands of rainbow-colored hair, her mouth quirks up in a half smile. She whispers something. Sylv tenses before she laughs, her voice rising above the crowd. "Contrary to popular opinion, I'm not looking forward to midterms."

Asha rolls her eyes. "*You* have nothing to worry about."

Sylv blushes, but Asha's right: Sylv's a straight-A student. The teachers adore her. She couldn't flunk an exam if she tried.

Asha turns to me, and that's my cue. I plaster on a fake smile. "Midterms aren't until next week. And I had better things to do than study over break."

"Philistine." Sylv sighs. "How do I put up with you?"

Because I'm yours.

The buttons on Asha's bag clink against each other. She flicks a purple lock of hair out of her face. "No stress? Lucky you."

Lucky me. Before I can say anything, Sylv beats me to it.

"So what *did* you do?"

"Nothing."

Around us, the drone of voices becomes louder, more

agitated. The first few moments after Trenton's speeches are always a mess, with everyone tumbling over each other trying to get out, but this is far more chaotic than usual.

A teacher pushes through. Probably to see what the holdup is.

Asha grins. "All of break? Absolutely nothing? C'mon, spill."

Sylv's eyes are soft and questioning, and I nibble on my lip. I don't want to let her down. "I found an old video recording of my mother's first *Swan Lake* in the attic this weekend. It was her audition for the Royal Ballet. She wasn't much older than me."

It's not salacious news, so I expect Asha to be disappointed, but she leans in closer. "Was it good?"

This surprises a smile out of me.

Opportunity High is a county high school, with students from all the small surrounding towns. Asha isn't one of us. She isn't Opportunity, where everyone knows everything about Mom and me. She isn't part of our home turf of familiar street names, churches, and shared secrets.

In Opportunity, everyone knows Mom danced around the world at every great company: London, Moscow, New York. She saw more countries than all of us combined. She told me about her travels and made me restless. For how much that memory of her hurts, watching her dance never does. "She was *amazing*."

Sylv's shoulder touches mine. Her warm smile anchors me. It's as if all of Opportunity falls away. We're lost between making a home and escaping one. It won't be long before our secrets choke us, before she finally realizes I don't deserve her and she leaves me too.

....

CLAIRE

After another lap, the crisp air becomes refreshing, though I'd never admit that to Coach. Winter ought to stick to December, to *Christmas*, and leave us be. We need as many hours as we can find to prepare for our next meet if we want to keep up our winning streak.

My JROTC drill team will start practice again soon too. It's only the youngest cadets' second year of training, and they're still finding their stride. I have enough on my mind without the frost.

I glance sideways to find Chris grinning at me. "What?"

"You're brooding."

"Am not."

He snorts.

"How was your break?" We ask the same question at the same time, and I laugh.

"It was weird not having Trace home for Matt's birthday, even though he's, quote, a high school student and all

17

grown up, so why do we worry so much?" My baby brother tries not to show how much this cold weather is hurting his joints or how much he misses our sister, who is far away in a foreign desert. All three of us, we've lost our flow. "We had a few minutes of video chat after you left."

"How is deployment treating her?"

I tread carefully. "Her patrols are uneventful. Just the way I like it."

Chris nods. His father, Lieutenant Colonel West, is preparing for his seventh tour. We both know what it's like to have part of your mind on the other side of the world, wondering what's happening in the sand and unforgiving heat. It's for the pride—and expectation—of our families that we serve.

Even me. And I would. If only I could be like Tracy, who is everything I want to be, everything I *should* be— brave, resilient, certain of herself. Everything I'm not.

"At least Matt hasn't had any fevers," I say after half a lap. It was the highlight of our winter break. Ever since Matt started at Opportunity, he's been doing better. The lupus still affects his joints, and most days he needs his crutches. But he's disguised them as lightsabers and claims they're for dueling. Jedi against JROTC. "He loves having his friends here. It made the start of the new year less daunting." *For all of us*, I add silently. It's good to know Matt's not alone.

"Will you talk to him about joining our cadets next year?" Chris asks. "To keep up tradition?"

"Of course." This conversation is another familiar rhythm, and I settle into it.

"Good. He still has three years. Opportunity wouldn't be the same without one of you in JROTC."

I muster a smile, though it probably resembles a grimace. *Next year. When I'm gone. When Chris is far away. When everything will be different, regardless of whether there's a Morgan in Opportunity's JROTC.*

"Are you looking forward to visiting West Point?" I ask after we turn to the long side of the track.

Chris shrugs. He was always a no-brainer for any military academy. We celebrated when he got his letter of assurance and his congressional nomination. It's everything he ever dreamed about.

But today he seems preoccupied too. On this first day of our last semester, the entire senior class is counting down to graduation. One school break left. One more summer before adulthood. Before we broke up, Tyler told me the best part of high school was getting out ASAP. Still, I wish it didn't have to end yet. It'll be hard to say good-bye to our team, to our cadets, to each other. Life will be grayer without seeing Chris all day, every day.

So we run. Not just in circles around the track. We run

toward all that is waiting for us. We run together while we still can.

....

SYLV

Autumn lingers. Her gray-and-blue eyes are conflicted, but those rare moments when she talks about her mother are like the dawn, and when she opens up, she is the sun. I don't want to see her hurt, but it's still better than watching her erect walls around herself.

My hand twitches by my side, itching to hold Autumn's. But I remain motionless so I won't spook her.

"She performed 'The Dying Swan,' which seems ironic now. She was young and careless and so…so fragile. I don't remember her like that. She always seemed so strong to me."

Only a few years after that audition, Joni Browne became principal dancer at the Royal Ballet. She was unconquerable, like Autumn was when she and her mother were together.

Around us, people grumble and wonder why we're not outside yet, but I want to hold on to this moment between classes a little longer.

"Do you know what you'll dance yet?" I prompt.

Asha perks up. "Oh, you're a dancer too! Are you auditioning already?"

Autumn glances at me sharply. She rarely talks about dancing anymore.

Don't worry, I mouth. Asha'll understand. She's good people.

Autumn's been training in the music room for *months* — and I've been sending out her applications. Her father may hate her for it, but I'd be a lousy girlfriend if I didn't see how much it meant to her. It's her chance out of here, and she deserves to be happy. Even though she can audition at schools closer to home or wait until she's a senior, she has her sights set on New York.

We both did once.

I stuff my hand in my pocket, and my fingers curl around the letter of admittance I've been carrying around for almost two weeks now.

"I'm auditioning for Juilliard," Autumn says quietly. "But I'm still deciding on my solo."

"My piano teacher always says there's no truer music than feeling," Asha shares.

She told me she wants to travel the world before she majors in music. She and Autumn could be friends if they only knew each other a little better. If only Autumn knew a *lot* of people a little better, maybe she wouldn't always be alone.

"He says music should have heartbreak and happiness, storm clouds and stars, as long as there's *emotion*. I think that's true for dance too."

Autumn lowers her guard and smiles in slow motion. "I've been thinking about dancing an original composition instead of something that's been choreographed for others. Before—when I still had lessons—Mom and I talked about it."

She never told *me* that. It's like the two of them are in their own universe, where everything around them glistens with the possibility of creation. And I'm left with bleak Opportunity and nothing more.

I inch toward the aisle. "There you go. You show them who you are and they can't say no."

Autumn half turns and grins, sending butterflies through my chest. "Tease." She sobers. "Have you heard from Brown yet?"

A freshman bumps into my elbow, and I let go of the letter. "No, not yet."

Because what can I tell her? That I have the ticket out of town she's been longing for? That I don't even know what to do with it? Before Mamá fell ill, I would've leaped at this chance. But how can I leave now?

Autumn would never understand.

She winces in sympathy. Asha grimaces.

In the row below ours, a flock of freshman girls giggle. Beside them, a boy frantically flips through a textbook while one of his friends rolls his eyes. All around us, people chatter about their breaks, classes, midterms.

If anyone wants to understand Opportunity—truly understand it—this moment between Principal Trenton's speech and class is the right time. The week has started, and there's no escaping it, but we start it together.

And soon—hopefully—we'll have fresh air to breathe.

Except we're all moving, but no one gets out.

To: Sis

I know you're at practice, but don't worry so much, okay? :) I like going to school. And I'm a lot tougher than I look.

To: Sis

(PS: The speech was totally the same. You could do it and no one would know the difference.)

CHAPTER THREE

AUTUMN

Asha got under my skin. Sylv doesn't understand dancing is more than a dream, more than a career path—it's my heartbeat. Asha *gets* it.

I wish I knew more about her, about her music. Before I can ask, we reach the aisle. The mass of students surrounds me and huddles closer with every step. Backpacks bump into me, shoulders touch. I'm not sure why no one is leaving the auditorium. There are too many people here.

My fingers curl around the charms on my bracelet: a silver ballet shoe and the handmade Venetian mask Mom brought back from Italy one year. The green paint on the mask has faded and the edges are worn off, but the familiar shapes are soothing and help me find my balance.

It's fleeting.

Asha gives me a shrug and a smile. "Good luck with your auditions," she calls, squeezing through the crowd. And she walks away.

Everyone does in the end.

I take a step back and wait for the crowd to pass me.

I have no friends here but Sylv, no family but a brother who disappears on me and a father who despises me. Only dancing keeps me alive. It will free me. And I can't let anything get in the way of that.

....

CLAIRE

The track opens up before us. After another lap, Chris's mood brightens. He's always been able to do that— throw off his worries like a winter coat. "Time to run. Have fun, Sarge."

I smirk. "Commander."

He winks and, as if he didn't just run a mile, pulls ahead, leaving me to stare at his back. Sure, he's a long-distance runner, so he's not even halfway through his rounds. But it only hammers home how ridiculously slow I am today.

That changes right now.

When I pass Coach again, I give him a small nod, and he punches the buttons on his stopwatch. I pick up the pace.

We've been working on this strategy since last season—build up my schedule so I can keep a stable pace through the better part of the race and still have enough left in me for a final half-track sprint.

26

Everything around me disappears. Every thought of Matt and Tracy. The burning pain in my calves. The nagging worry of managing drill meets and JROTC. My three teammates, who are each on their own stretch of the track, working on their own personal records.

Everything disappears but the cadence of my feet and the cold air on my cheeks.

When I'm running, I can finally breathe.

I sprint across the finish line and look over to see Coach grin.

The bleachers beside the track are covered in a white haze. At the steps near the finish line, someone has scratched WE MAKE HISTORY into the wood.

A smile tugs at my lips. Those three words are Coach Lindt's take on our school motto. His *Any Given Sunday* motivational speech. And it works because we *have* made history, and I don't doubt we'll be competing in the state championships for the seventh year in a row.

This is my team. This is where I belong.

Here and now, we are everyone.

....

TOMÁS

When the file doesn't give me any answers, I shove it back and slam the drawer shut for good measure. Pointless.

Ridiculous. Just plain stupid. Tyler's reenrolling and my sister's terrified, but I do not know why. There's absolutely nothing I can do to make her feel better.

"How about we skip the rest of the day?" Fareed leans against the door frame, one foot propped up on a visitor's chair. He uses the tip of his folder to push a strand of hair out of his face. "I hate Mondays."

I drop the role of protective brother and shrug back into my guise as Opportunity High's most infamous student. It fits me like a well-worn glove. "Dude, we all do. Mondays are the worst. But I'm working on my tough-guy image. If I don't suffer with the rest of you, it'd ruin my rep."

"C'mon, admit it. You're just afraid Trenton will tell your grandfather. What's the worst he can do? Beat you up for cutting? You know the old man doesn't mind."

I stretch. "I guess."

The thing is, I *am* afraid. When Fareed moved here, I was Opportunity's favorite bad boy. No one actually told me that, but I can only assume they were blinded by my brilliance.

This year, we share that dubious honor, and only Far knows I've been tiptoeing the lines. Admittedly, a day without detention is like a day without sunshine. Or rainbows or kittens or that sort of crap. But I do my homework. I maintain shockingly decent grades. Principal Trenton and I have come to an agreement: I don't break the rules too much and don't skip my classes. I don't get caught pulling stunts, like breaking into school records— even for my sis, though she's worth the risk. I behave and Trenton won't call home to Granddad.

Not because I'm worried about his anger or his disappointment. Hell, I'm head and shoulders taller than he is; he's not that intimidating.

I'm afraid he'll tell Mamá. And I don't want her to remember me like this.

....

SYLV

My hand grazes Autumn's wrist as I move down the row of seats to try to see what's going on at the back of the auditorium. She hates it when we touch in public, but these past couple of months, she's been the only one keeping me standing. She's so set on leaving Opportunity that I think she'll tear me in two when she does.

I wish I could leave too. I wish I could stay.

The students around me are motionless, and the buzz has deepened to a murmur of unease. *Something's wrong. What's happening? Locked. The doors are locked.*

One of the cheerleaders grumbles that this isn't the time for jokes. A few seats away from her, a freshman laughs nervously. At the end of every aisle, students crowd around the double doors that would normally swing open but today don't budge. Near the stage, someone shouts that the emergency exit is locked too. We're locked in.

The bell rings.

One set of doors to my left opens. Fluorescent light filters in around a lone figure. For a moment, I think it's my twin brother, finding yet another way to prove he is the least interested, most interesting student at Opportunity. It's the kind of prank he'd pull, locking us all in. It's something I'd have done with him. Once.

But blond locks peek out from under a black knit cap. Strangely, that's the first thing I notice—the unruly blond hair that frames that too-familiar face. And with it come the memories. A wild grin. A dangerous hunger. The nervous whispers around me may as well come from my own mind. *Not now. Not today. Not yet.*

No, please.

It takes me a second to process his raised arm.

At the top of the aisles, everyone pauses and all eyes turn toward the shadow in the doorway. The word "gun" floats all around me before the crowd silences, stills. I don't feel panic or shock. There's just a sense of defeat.

This is it.

"Principal Trenton, I have a question." The figure points the weapon at her, and his finger curls around the trigger.

Then he fires.

The Adventures of Mei

Current location: Home

>> Opportunity always looks the same. A little bit smaller compared with Jinan and my grandparents'. A little bit grayer once you've been to the other side of the world. But no matter where I go, it's nice to come home. And even nicer to not have to go to school anymore.

Now to catch up on mail, chocolate, and the start of the day.

Comments: <0>

CHAPTER FOUR

TOMÁS

Once I've returned the files to the filing cabinet, I pick up a glass paperweight and toy with it, tossing it high and snatching it out of the air. I wander toward the principal's door and inch it open, staring out of the administrative office's glass walls.

When the bell rings, I wait for the hallways to fill up. Trenton's speech should be over, and no one stays in the auditorium longer than necessary.

But the halls remain empty, as if we're the only two people in the building.

This silence spooks me. "Far?"

He glances up from double-checking his test scores — not like they'll get any better. "What?"

I open my mouth and close it again. What do I say to him? It's too quiet? "Put the file away. We should go before Trenton gets back."

Dude. *Weak*.

I slip into the administrative office, where the secretary's computer still glows blue, set on the lock screen. A framed picture of a cat stands next to the keyboard. I flip the paperweight up high and catch it again. The mindless repetition is comforting. "Far, *c'mon*."

Where is *everyone?*

Toss. Catch.

Toss.

Two loud cracks tear through the air. The paperweight slips out of my hands, breaking into a thousand shards on the floor.

"What was that?" Fareed appears in the doorway, still holding on to his file.

I don't—I can't—"What the fuck was that?" Far repeats, louder. Though he knows—we both do. We've spent time hunting with my granddad and my sister. We've watched plenty of movies. Far grew up in a war zone. We both know the sound of gunshots.

But it can't be. It can't happen. Not here.

"We need to get out," Far says. "Warn someone." Despite his haunted eyes, his voice is clear and steady. It makes him sound older.

I nod—before the silence around us hits me like a sledgehammer. I know the hallways are supposed to be empty. We spent hours practicing lockdown drills. But no one sounded the alarm. No one ran to cover.

No one appeared in the hallways at all. I shake my head. "No."

No. No. No. Fuck no.

Everyone is still in the auditorium. Everyone including my sister. I have to get to her.

I can't fail her again.

....

SYLV

Tyler is back. Tyler is back.

Tyler is back.

The refrain pounds in my brain as loudly as the next shots sound in the auditorium. *Tyler is back.* The words make me want to vomit or hide under my seat. I freeze in terror, as I did all those months ago.

I don't know what to do. I don't know where to run. Autumn and I are one aisle over and only a few rows down from where Tyler stands. Too far up to bolt for the wings. Too far down to make for the doors. Too anything.

Around us, the room is swept up in panic. Screams echo in my ears. Teachers standing near the doors try to approach Tyler, but he picks them off methodically, like everyone who gets too close. At every shot, I flinch. We're not close enough to see the teachers' faces, and

I'm almost grateful. He *shot* them. *Ah, Dios. This can't be real*.

Students clamber to the other doors, pushing forward, but no one is leaving.

Tyler is back.

People run down the rows of seats, shouting for help. Two students—a boy and a girl, both from one of the outer towns—are splayed across the chairs in front of Tyler. The boy still has his bag half slung over his shoulder as his blood mixes with hers.

I can't move.

I can't breathe.

The stage is a mess of people congregating around Principal Trenton—teachers, Trenton's secretary. Mr. Jameson, everyone's favorite English teacher, crouches next to the principal and tries to stem the blood flow, except she's hit in the head, and it's not blood but brains.

Behind them, several members of Opportunity's chorus flee toward the wings, where the dressing rooms and the lighting control system are. Ms. Smith, the elderly librarian, sneaks toward the second emergency exit at the side of the auditorium. Or rather, she walks tenderly because she had a hip replacement last year. With her back to Tyler, she seems fearless.

She's seventy-three. Her youngest daughter is pregnant again and her oldest grandkid turns eleven today.

She's lived in the same house on the same street since the dawn of time.

She brought Mamá freshly baked bread yesterday, just like she does every Sunday. She made me chicken soup when everyone thought I was ill.

No. No. No. No.

Dios te salve, Maria, llena eres de gracia: el Señor es contigo. Bendita tú eres entre todas las mujeres y bendito—

My eyes are drawn back to Tyler. His hair color is so much like Autumn's, it makes me sick.

Remember me.

I've never been able to forget him.

He scans the crowd. He keeps close to the doorway, and everyone pushes away from him. He holds the gun with confidence. Tyler is too determined, too accurate. Even Abuelo would not be able to teach him anything.

He points his weapon at the librarian. Fires.

She crumples steps from the door.

With his free hand, he pushes a stray strand of hair back under his cap.

Autumn moves in front of me, as if she wants to protect me, but I should be protecting her.

Dios te salve, Maria… The words taste foreign on my tongue. I can't remember what comes next. I'm trembling all over, and I can't stop.

Next to me, a freshman girl stumbles down the row

of seats. One of the jocks hoists her up by her arms, but there's nowhere to go. She screams and pounds her fists against his chest. He wraps his arms around her.

Autumn turns her head toward me, but while her mouth moves, I can't hear her.

All I can see is Principal Trenton's surprised smile as she was shot and the horror of the people around who rushed to help her. I hear gasps and cries and screams. There's death, there's dying, and there's blood everywhere.

Tyler is back.

....

CLAIRE

The second shot rings out at 10:05 a.m. Almost comically, Coach stares at the starting gun in his hand, as if it fired without his noticing. But the sound didn't come from him; it came from inside the school.

Another shot. More shots. My heart beats to match their erratic rhythm.

Closest to the school, Chris crosses the dozen or so yards between him and the double doors of the gym before any of us can react. He rattles the handles to no avail, kicks against the door, and I'm not sure if his anger is pain or desperation.

The cold air seeps through my skin and chills me to

the bone. All I can think about is how if Chris strains a muscle, it will ruin his last season before it has even started. Our season. Our team. All four of us. Anything beyond that—anything to make sense of what we're hearing—is too much.

For a second or two, everything is still. Only our breaths cloud the air. Then Esther starts to sob. When she reaches the finish line, Avery wraps an arm around her shoulders.

We're waiting for someone to take the lead. We turn our attention to Coach, who has produced the keys to the gym. But the doors won't budge, either because they're jammed or locked from the inside. Coach is pale and silent.

We turn our attention to Chris. But he stares at me with a plea in his eyes.

I freeze. I know how to follow orders—follow *others*— but Trace was always the one in control, both at JROTC and at home. I don't like being in command. Still, she taught me the drills. *C'mon, C, you can do it*. Even Tyler once told me I could be so much more.

And if something's happening inside the school, Matt needs me.

I breathe in deeply to keep the burning bile down. I square my shoulders and sprint toward the others, patting my leggings out of habit, looking for the phone I left in our locker room.

"We need to call 911. Does anyone have their phone?"

No one answers.

"Coach?"

Coach is supposed to have a cell for emergencies, but he still hasn't made it out of the last century—and no one has ever minded. This is Opportunity. Nothing ever happens here.

"Where are the nearest emergency phones?" I ask.

Coach grunts. "There's one at the main entrance to the school."

Opportunity High School moved to a new location five years ago—after the original school was swept up to Oz by a tornado. The new building is state of the art—larger sports fields, fancy equipment, right in the middle of fuck all. I *loved* it. It felt like home. Until now.

"There's a pay phone at the gas station down the road too," I remember. "And we can find Jonah."

Blank stares.

"The security guard." My teammates probably never bothered to learn his name, never spent quiet afternoons hanging out in his patrol car. "He should be in the parking lot. He has a radio and will be able to help. We'll split into groups. Coach, go find the emergency phone. Stay safe. Stay away from the school."

Coach nods slowly. Normally, we follow him or Chris, our team captain. But Coach's planning never extended beyond the borders of our training field. He listens to me, despite the fact that my voice trembles and cracks.

"Esther, Avery." I turn to the girls. They're usually talkative but not now. "Find out if any of the emergency exits open, but stay away from the windows. If you can get in, find a phone. If not, figure out how to hot-wire a car. I don't care what you do, but alert anyone and everyone.

"The two of us"—I point to Chris and me—"we'll find Jonah. If he's not out front, we'll run to the gas station for help." I breathe in sharply. "We don't know what's happening inside, but if the situation sounds like a shooting and looks like a shooting, treat it as a shooting. We need emergency responders here as soon as possible."

Chris nods. "It's a good plan," he says. Those four words are enough to set everyone into motion, but I also hear his unspoken promise. *We're in this together. Always.* He'll follow me, like I'll follow him. It's why we need each other close.

Avery and Esther pick up their water bottles and start running. Coach follows, dazed.

Chris tosses me my sports drink, and I take a few gulps before discarding it.

More shots break the icy air, and we run.

....

40

AUTUMN

Sylv screams. Her hands are cold in mine as I pull her close. Her eyes flick from left to right. A few steps above us, on the other side of the aisle, Asha has dropped her books. She's wrapped her arms around her waist, and despite all the color she wears, she shrinks into herself. At the next shot, she recoils. As if instinctively, she moves back to us.

Students mass together to get away from Tyler. They climb over the seats to get to the far side of the auditorium, where the throng is just as heavy.

The doors to the hallway are locked. It seems the emergency exists are disabled too. The doors behind the stage only lead to dressing rooms and the prop room.

There's no way out.

Down by the stage, the unlucky few hide between their seats or shiver in the aisles. Teachers and a handful of students drag the wounded behind chairs for protection. The chorus members who made a beeline backstage have not reappeared, but few would risk running out in the open to cross the elevated stage.

All the while, Tyler stands in the doorway, protected by the walls around him and the gun in his hands. He doesn't move. He doesn't have to—he has the high ground. He leans back. He lets terror overtake us and shoots whoever comes too close.

The shooter.

Two words that taste sour and foreign. *My brother.*

I bite the inside of my cheek and focus on the pain. Ty reenrolled to finish his senior year. He was supposed to talk through his options with Trenton today. He was supposed to put things right.

My brother, who cared for my bruises when Dad couldn't contain his grief. Who helped me dance in secret. My fingers wrap around the ballet charm. Even after everything he's done, he is my home.

Once, he caught Dad's belt on his bare arm to stop it from coming down on me. Afterward, Tyler cracked a joke and tousled my hair. He is the only real family I have.

It can't be him.

And today of all days.

I should get up. I should reason with him.

But he holds a gun, and his eyes flash dangerously. Sylv clings to me. We crouch low. From between the seats, I can see the body of one of our classmates. Her face is obscured by someone's book bag, and blood pools on the floor. "We have to move," I manage.

Neither Asha nor Sylv reacts at first. After what seems an eternity, Asha nods. She bends down to pick up her books, then stops and stares. No point in lugging them around now. They won't be able to shield her.

A strangled cry swirls up from the lowest rows of the auditorium.

Carefully, I get to my feet. I tug at Sylv's sleeve. She doesn't give any indication of feeling it. As long as the commotion distracts Tyler, I want to take advantage of it. "Come on. We have to get away from here."

I glance back toward my brother.

In the aisle adjacent to ours, leading up to Tyler, I recognize a petite girl with braces and too-large glasses. Geraldine. She's a freshman. I only know her because she practices her singing in the music room. Her hands are curled into fists. She sways back and forth, physically indecisive, then she sprints up the aisle, toward the door.

She throws herself in a leap—a grand jeté—and I can see myself dance like her. She moves with delicacy.

The bullet picks her straight out of the air.

She stumbles and falls. Another freshman spurts forward, maybe in an attempt to help her, then skids to a halt as Tyler fires another shot—this time at the clock above the stage.

He smiles. "Please stay where you are."

A terrified silence descends upon the auditorium. We're all captives now.

CJ Johnson

@CadetCJJ

GUN. HELP. #OHS

10:06 AM

Alex Saxon

@AlexDoesTwitter

@CadetCJJ For real? There's nothing on the news... #OHS

10:06 AM

George Johnson

@G_Johnson1

@CadetCJJ ARE YOU OK? TELL ME YOU'RE OK.

10:06 AM

George Johnson

@G_Johnson1

@CadetCJJ ARE YOU SERIOUS? I'M CALLING 911.

10:07 AM

Abby Smith
@YetAnotherASmith
@CadetCJJ @G_Johnson1 George, I'm
driving over right now #OHS

10:07 AM

16 favorites 2 retweets

Anonymous
@BoredOpportunist
@CadetCJJ I know Mondays are BORING
but you're sick. #hoax #OHS

10:07 AM

15 retweets

George Johnson
@G_Johnson1
@YetAnotherASmith @CadetCJJ
NOT SURE THAT'S WISE. LET THE
PROFESSIONALS DEAL.

10:07 AM

Jay Eyck
@JEyck32
@CadetCJJ Whats going on? #OHS

10:07 AM

CHAPTER FIVE

TOMÁS

The sunlight filters in through the window. The shards of the glass paperweight cast rainbows on the walls. Fareed strides to the secretary's desk. He's paler than me now, and I can't even joke about it.

He locks the door to the administrative office, cutting us off from the hallways, before he picks up the phone and dials 911. I hover by the desk, unable to stand still. If it were my decision, I'd make straight for the auditorium to convince myself this is a joke we happened to be on the wrong side of—convince myself this is a normal Monday morning.

Only Fareed's rationality stops me. I never claimed to be the brains in this partnership. I'm here for bad ideas and impulsivity.

I turn on my heel and ram my fist into one of the supply cabinets. The thin board splinters on impact, cutting my knuckles, but the pain offers no relief.

"What has that cabinet ever done to you?" Fareed asks me.

On the other side of the line, something clicks and a muffled voice reaches through the receiver.

I still.

"I'm calling from Opportunity High," Fareed says after giving our names. "We've heard gunshots." He sounds so calm. The Fareed I know, with his steadily teasing smile, has disappeared. I've never met this Fareed. He articulates with care so his Afghan accent isn't as pronounced. Next thing, they'll mark him as a suspect. It wouldn't be the first time. Things happen in the school, and he gets questioned even when it doesn't concern him at all. I hate it. It's so unfair—but at least it gives me some downtime.

The voice mumbles something unintelligible, and Fareed answers. "We've heard several shots. I don't know if anyone is hurt." He listens for a moment. "No, no, we're not hurt."

I inch a little closer, but I can imagine the operator's next questions. *Where are you? How many of you are there?*

"Just the two of us. We're in the principal's office. The rest of the students and the teachers are in the auditorium for an assembly. The shots seemed to come from over there. We haven't been to the back of the school. No, we won't. We heard footsteps right before the shooting but nothing else."

Can you get out? That's what I would ask, but the voice relays more information. It's almost comforting to listen. The low murmur from the phone line and the occasional gunfire in the distance are the only sounds. We're safe here. I think.

"Yes, yes. The principal's office is in the administrative wing. On the east side of the building. First floor. The principal's parking spot is outside the window. It's clearly marked."

I smile without mirth. The principal's parking spot used to be toward the auditorium, with the rest of the faculty, but my oldest brother once spray-painted Trenton's car pink after the two of them got into an, uh, educational disagreement. She moved the parking spot so she could keep an eye on her new convertible.

"We've locked the door. We haven't seen or heard anyone else. We don't know what the situation is like in the rest of the building."

Gunshots. Threats. Deaths.

"We can get out through the window if we have to."

It won't have been the first time we've sneaked out but never like this.

I strain to hear the response on the phone. I don't want to leave this office when I don't know what's waiting for me outside.

"Yes, I think it will be safe. If we walk south, we won't be in range of the auditorium."

Fareed stares at me while he listens to the instructions. He shakes his head, and I can imagine what they're saying. *Run if you can. Hide if you have to. Don't be a target.* It's the first thing all the instructors of our lockdown drills taught us: get yourself to safety.

But what they failed to tell us is that running away and saving your own skin is only noble when you don't leave anyone behind. If I were in the auditorium, I'd want someone to come for me. I'd want there to be hope.

"Yes, we'll open the window and wait outside. Do you need me to stay on the line?" Fareed's hand trembles, and he nods at me once more before he says, "Okay, okay. We'll wait outside. Thank you."

....

SYLV

All sounds—all shouts—fade. My vision blurs, as if the connection between me and the rest of the world has been severed. The air is stale. It hurts to breathe.

Autumn's whispers tug at me as her hands pull at my arm. I want to reach out to her. *Hold me. Keep me safe.* I am frozen.

But Tyler's voice teases me. I cannot—I *do* not—want to deal with it. Not here. Not now. Not ever.

49

All my worries rush over me. Mamá's empty eyes. Abuelo struggling to keep the farm running while caring for her. My older brothers asking me questions I can't answer: *Where will you be next year? What do you want to do? How are you?*

When I close my eyes, all I see are the faces of the two people who mean the most to me—the two people I both cling to and push away. My good-for-nothing, perfect-for-me brother, who somehow managed to get sent to the principal's office during the very first period of the first day of the semester. He's out there somewhere. I hope. I pray.

And Autumn. Always, always Autumn.

Tyler drove a wedge between all of us, though I could never tell them about it. Tomás would've torn him apart for me, and it would've destroyed what little family Autumn has left.

The only things that give us purpose are the stories that tie us together. We all have so many secrets to keep. And I hold mine close. Before my junior year and her sophomore year, Autumn led me to an abandoned shed, the only remnant of a farm that once stood there, outside the town border. We'd meet between the cornfields every evening and share the day's gossip from neighbors, who always seemed to know everything going on in Opportunity.

Last summer, the large shed began to double as her

studio. Hidden in a blanket of gold under the thick August air, time was ours. During the day, she was whoever she wanted to be. When we were together, she showed me what dancing felt like.

Until one evening, everything changed for good.

The corn plumes seemed to be ablaze in the setting sun, and the high stalks kept prying eyes at bay. I worked on my college applications and watched tufts of early cotton float on the wind while Autumn danced. I didn't know what I wanted to major in yet—I didn't even know for sure I wanted *to go to college. Not while Mamá was getting worse every day. But for Autumn's sake, I filled out the forms. We'd always planned to go together.*

"Do you think the two of you sneaking out every night goes unnoticed? I thought I'd made myself clear."

I startled at the sound of the voice, and when I saw whom it belonged to, my blood ran cold.

I hadn't seen Tyler since junior prom, when he pinned me against a wall and told me I was corrupting Autumn. He fiercely protected his sister from threats the rest of Opportunity didn't see or, in the case of their dad, didn't want to see. He didn't trust anyone. It made him unpredictable, dangerous, and better left alone.

"Go away, Tyler."

"You're trespassing. You can't tell me to go away."

"Back off." I picked up my books from underneath the

tree and stuffed them into my backpack. "Or go inside if you want to watch Autumn dance."

Tyler is the spitting image of his sister—or rather, the other way around. They have the same straw-colored hair: his tucked behind his ears, hers still a little longer back then. With his suede jacket and his polished boots, he looked older than his seventeen years and beautiful, in a classic sort of way.

The corners of his mouth curled into a slow smile. His hungry once-over made me cringe.

I didn't wait for his answer but slung the bag over my shoulder. "Tell Autumn I'll see her tomorrow."

I walked toward the edge of the cotton field, but Tyler followed me. He wasn't even subtle about it. He whistled some happy tune while his footsteps crossed my shadow and his breath tickled the back of my neck.

"I cared about her dancing once. Before you took her away from me."

"I didn't take anyone away from anyone," I snapped.

He traced my arm with his nail. "Don't lie to me. You corrupted my sister." He placed his hands on my shoulders again, his thumbs digging into my neck.

"I don't know what you're talking about." I jerked, attempting to dislodge his grip, but he only squeezed harder. I reached back, scratching at his hands and hoped against hope that Autumn had heard his voice, would

come looking for us. Maybe she would not dance all night. Maybe she wouldn't forget time.

She always did.

I dropped my bag and tried to stomp on his foot. He spun me by my arm. I stumbled, crashing to the plowed earth.

He swept my feet from under me when I tried to get up. "This thing *between you and Autumn, it's a disease. It's not natural. You think you can come into our lives and steal my family. You need someone to set you right."*

"Your family?" I shot back, despair strengthening my voice. "When is the last time you took an interest in Autumn? You don't know the first thing about family."

When I tried to roll over and crawl away from him, his boot found my stomach, and I doubled over. He pinned me, his knees on my arms and his hands on my shirt. When he leaned down, his breath smelled sour. "They abandoned me. They all did." His grin stole the scream from my lungs. His finger traced my jawline. I couldn't move.

"Next time your brother tries to get in my way, I will kill him. Remember that." Tyler hovered above me while the sky turned purple. "And I will make sure you remember me."

I couldn't run then. I couldn't escape, no matter how hard I tried. I've been running ever since.

"Remember."

And now he's found me.

....

53

CLAIRE

"Thank you," Chris says as soon as we're out of earshot from the rest of the group.

My breathing is shallow. Running on the hard concrete rattles my knees.

Although I don't need an explanation for Chris's hesitation, he gives one anyway. "School was always supposed to be safe." He grasps for words. "I—"

I nod. "I know." *Nothing ever happens here.*

Cars fill up the student parking lot, even though most of us take the bus to school. The route to and from Opportunity High is a single two-lane road. Behind the school's athletic fields, there is a forest, but in front of the school, the fields stretch out as far as the eye can see. Somewhere in the distance is civilization. Here, there is just flat, open land with a slate-gray sky overhead.

Two cars sit at the entrance to the parking lot, Jonah's patrol car one of them. The white paint's so dusty, it's almost gray, and scratches cross the navy-blue school logo. I spent many hours in its front seat, my knees propped against the dashboard, munching away at one of the chocolate muffins Jonah brought to share.

We met by accident last year when I missed the late bus home after Mom called to tell me Matt had been rushed to the hospital. Jonah got permission to drive me into the city. We talked the whole way, and his outrageous anecdotes were the pick-me-up I needed.

When I thanked him a couple days later, we talked more. He told me he wasn't supposed to let students in his car because it could be seen as inappropriate. But he smiled before he protested, and it didn't sound very vehement. Eventually, I wore him down.

After Matt was released from the hospital, he gave me one of his figurines to give to Jonah. It found a place of pride on his dashboard, and I found a place to get away to think—away from Matt's precarious health and my sister's deployment, away from Chris, away from all the expectations. Jonah and I simply talked.

It makes me feel safer now, knowing Jonah is close. Most students ignored Jonah. Parents grumbled about the invasion of privacy. But Jonah once told me he never minded being disliked as long as he could do his duty. I wish I felt the same.

I slow to a trot, circling the car. From the outside, I can see it's empty. A paper cup from the local bakery sits on the dashboard. "J?"

A second car is parked haphazardly across three parking spaces. This car I once knew as well as I know Jonah's.

"Claire?" Chris calls. "Isn't this—"

"Yes..." My voice trails off.

It's been a while since I saw Ty, particularly because

he dropped out, but I always expected him to come back. He cares too much about his education. He prides himself on following the rules even when others don't, no matter how ridiculous those rules might be. It's not like him to leave his car like this, but the muddy brown hood is popped. "Looks like his car broke down. They must've gone to find help or get another set of jumper cables."

I breathe. *Ty's back. We're less alone.*

Despite everything that happened, Ty's good people. Breakup or not, he always believed in me. He still smiles when he sees me in his father's store. He always asks about Matt.

If he's inside, he'll protect Matt. And if he arrived after Trenton's speech, he'll be able to help us.

He has to help us.

Chris takes the lead once more, and I comfortably fall into step.

"Then why wouldn't one of them stay here? Why wouldn't they take Jonah's car?" Chris asks. He edges to the passenger door, but Ty's car is locked. "Does Jonah have a mobile radio?"

I open the door to Jonah's car and peek in. The cold air closes in on me. His transceiver's missing. The wiring around the base station is cut. My heart slams into my throat. "Chris?"

I turn around, but Chris has his face pressed against the

window. He's as white as the frost on the grass. "Claire, there are ammo boxes in here."

"What?" I walk toward him and kick a shoe. I've inadvertently kicked my teammates' shoes all the time during warm-ups, so I don't even look down—not immediately.

"Gun cases too," Chris says, continuing to take inventory.

I look to see what almost tripped me. Time moves in bursts today, cranking up to be impossibly fast, screeching to become painfully slow. And now it stops altogether.

Jonah's boots—Jonah's feet—protrude from under the car.

I crouch down, and when my fingers brush his socks, his ankles are cold. I place an arm on the concrete and lean to look under the car. There's blood on the ground.

In the shadows of the car, Jonah lies at an unnatural angle. Empty eyes stare at me.

I stifle a scream. Chris's voice trembles when he says, "Claire, I don't think anything happened to Tyler. I think Tyler is happening to us."

....

AUTUMN

Fear and survival are two sides of the same coin. Dad taught me that. These last two years, he proved it again and again and again. Terror is our strongest force because we're only afraid when we have something to lose—our lives, our loves…our dignity.

It's been such a long time since I felt afraid.

But now Ty is here. My brother. My Tyler. His smile belies his gun, and we're all enthralled by it. Despite being a thousand against one, we are powerless.

What would Dad say about that?

"Come here." I draw Sylv close and whisper assurances in her ear. Her eyes are wild, and tears stream down her face. She whimpers unintelligible words, but she responds to my touch. Her breathing eases—as if her mind's slipping someplace safe. Wherever it is, I hope she stays there.

"Follow me. Trust me." I curl my fingers around her wrist and gently pull. Everyone knows Ty. Knows me. We need to move.

The mood in the auditorium shifts.

Dancing teaches you how to read people from the way they hold themselves, the way their hands clench when they're scared, the grand motions they make when they're excited. The threats and yearning in a stolen glance and the brazen gestures of fear and fight and despair.

"Sylv." I pull her through our section of seats, toward the farthest corner from Ty, not waiting for Asha to make the same trek. Behind the last row of seats, we still cannot hide. The stares of those around us burn.

The fingers of my free hand push the ballet shoe charm deep into my palm.

Ty steps forward, and the door shuts behind him. As if we are in a vacuum, the silence in the auditorium intensifies. The world outside might cease to exist and we wouldn't notice.

Tyler pulls a lock from his pocket and tosses it to a sandy-haired boy standing nearest to him—a skinny kid who almost drops it. "Be so kind as to lock this door."

The boy trembles. He takes a step, moving slowly, as if the lock weighs him down. He hesitates, and the next shot drills through his shoulder.

"NOW." Ty's voice echoes through the auditorium. "If you please."

The boy cradles his arm against his body. He stumbles.

Students stare. *We* stare. We do not help. We do not fight. I don't speak up. It's self-preservation.

The boy starts to crumple, and a mousy-haired girl reaches out to steady him. I think her name's CJ. She's a junior too.

She glances at Ty and the gun. Everyone else who came too close has been shot. Tyler nods, graciously giving his approval. I guess it doesn't matter who locks us in as long as someone does.

CJ supports the boy as he weaves the chain with the lock through the door's handles. Their hands touch as the padlock clicks shut.

We're trapped.

The key tumbles onto the crimson carpet. CJ reaches down to grab it, as if by reflex, then freezes.

Ty beckons with the gun. "Bring it to me."

She eyes the weapon and does not hesitate. We all hold our breaths to see what will happen to her.

Nothing.

He holds out his hand, accepts the key, and allows her to walk back to the boy she helped.

Ty's voice fills the auditorium once more, his tone as casual as if he were discussing the frosty weather. "I have no issue with most of you, so I'd rather you don't force me to waste my bullets."

He's comfortable with our fear. He's feeding off of it. This—this is calculation: the gun, the locks, the date, the deaths. He has a carefully structured plan.

My brother has always had a flair for the dramatic.

Jay Eyck
@JEyck32

Gun? WTF? #OHS

10:07 AM

Jay Eyck
@JEyck32

Some1 tell me whats happening over at #OHS

10:08 AM

Jay (@JEyck32) ➔ Kevin (@KeviiinDR)

Dude, whats going on there? DM me back?!

10:08 AM

CHAPTER SIX

SYLV

The memories overwhelm me, and I wish I could forget like Mamá. But the present isn't any better.

The silence from the auditorium is tense and loaded. Except it's not silence. All around me there are hushed sobs, prayers, and curses—friends trying to calm each other: "Hold on to my hand." "Trust me." "We'll make it through."

People whisper into cell phones: "Help me." "I don't know what to do." "We've got to fight. We've got to take him down."

It's an endless current of fear, and Tyler revels in the power. He's the only one who does not feel lost right now.

A cheerleader sits cross-legged on the floor, between two rows of seats. Her bag lies in her lap, and she toys with a key chain attached to it. All the while, tears trickle down her cheeks.

My hand creeps toward the phone in my bag. For the

first time in months, I want to hear my brother's voice. But if he doesn't pick up—if Tyler found him—it will kill me.

The kid in the row in front of us doesn't share my hesitations.

"Mom? No, no, I can't speak up... Mom, you have to listen to me... There's someone in the school." His voice trembles. "No, I mean with a gun. There's someone with a gun in the school."

Tyler *with a gun*, I mentally correct. *Not just someone*. Tyler.

He strides down the aisle, toward the stage, apparently oblivious to the students who plot to stop him. He glances around, noting faces. Everyone keeps their distance, which gives him the upper hand.

"No, Mom. *Mom*. It isn't *one of those friends of mine*. Did you hear me? We can't get out. We're locked inside. CJ is okay. I thought he was going to shoot her. She's somewhere on the other side of the auditorium." His voice breaks. I reach out to nudge him to be quiet. He'll attract attention. He can't help his CJ if he's dead. "Mom, I'm so scared."

Halfway down the aisle, Tyler fires a bullet into the ceiling. "Hasn't anyone ever told you people how rude it is to be on the phone when someone is speaking?" He spins on his heel and pans the back of the auditorium. No matter what stands between us, I'm convinced his eyes find mine, like they always do. No matter where I go, no matter how far I run, I can never hide from him.

A smile tugs at his lips before he resumes his walk.

The boy in front of me whimpers. His phone slides from his slack hands, down under the seats. The voice on the other side fades.

....

CLAIRE

"No." No, there has to be another explanation why Jonah is lying dead under Ty's car. His sister borrowed Ty's car. There was an accident. "Not Ty. It can't be him." *Please*.

Chris pulled Jonah close to check his vitals signs, but he shakes his head and closes Jonah's eyes. His gaze is troubled as he reaches out to me, but I back away.

"Claire…"

"No, it can't be. I *know* Ty."

"Are you sure about that?" Chris asks. "All the evidence points to the contrary."

"Don't you trust me?"

"I don't trust *him*. He was never good for you."

Ty is a sore point between us. He always has been, and everything inside me rebels—against Chris, against this situation, against my better judgment. "You don't get to decide that for me."

Chris steps toward me. "He lied to you."

I cannot accept this is Ty's doing. He believed in me when no one else did. He loved me. He may not always have been true, but he never lied to me.

"Forget it," I bite out. We have no time for this right now. Hopefully Coach will have gotten to the emergency phone, but if that isn't the case, we need to act. "We need to get to the gas station. We need to get help."

"We could take Jonah's car," Chris suggests.

I didn't check to see if the keys were still in the ignition, but the thought of using the car with Jonah lying— with Jonah gone? I *can't*.

I have to get out. Out. Out. Out.

The sound of my footsteps on the concrete creates a soothing rhythm. And the road stretches out before me.

One two three four. One two three four. I keep count, like Coach would on the track.

One two three four.

One.

Two.

Three.

Four.

Chris falls into step behind me. I tense. But with the pace set, my mind is free to wander.

"You know you don't have to follow in your sister's footsteps, right? You could be more—so much more. Opportunity doesn't know how precious you are. Opportunity doesn't know a lot of things." Ty stroked the palm of my hand. With my head against his chest, the words rumbled in my ear. *"I won't let the army steal my girl and force her to be someone she doesn't want to be. You have dreams you should follow."*

I gazed up at him. The black circle around his eye, souvenir of yet another fight, showed how little Opportunity cared about his *dreams. I knew his scars ran deeper than the bruises. But with me, he felt safe—and I with him.*

We sat in his car just outside the school grounds and stared at the empty road—the same road Chris and I are running down. Opportunity is a sleepy town. Some days, the only traffic these streets see are the cars going back and forth to Opportunity High. Even the gas station is half-deserted and overgrown, with tumbleweeds and all. Matt used to call it a superhero headquarters in disguise.

Ty once promised to take Matt there after-hours, since Mr. Browne owns both the gas station and the hardware store on Main. Ty planned to tell Matt ghost stories and give him all the candy he could eat. And Matt would've loved it. He admired Ty as much as Ty loved hanging out with him.

But that was before junior prom, before the breakup.

That day though, Ty still held me. We were oblivious to the future that was waiting for us.

"What is my dream then?" I asked. Trace and I'd shared the same dream for so long, it seemed almost ludicrous to think of some other fate.

Ty wrapped his arms tighter around me. "I always thought you should teach. You love being with the underclassmen, and they look up to you." He leaned forward and kissed the top of my head. "Besides, it'll keep you closer to me."

"Cheeky." I poked Ty in his ribs. "And what do you dream about? Taking over your father's store?"

"Maybe."

"You know you could go anywhere, be anyone you want."

"I know." He paused. "I want us to build a home together."

"Here in Opportunity?"

"One of the abandoned farms at the outskirts of town. It'll be quiet there. And protected. Somewhere we'll both be safe."

I smiled sadly, not wanting to deny him his dream. Almost everyone in our class talked about leaving Opportunity, but even though Ty wasn't happy here, he never did. Sometimes it felt as if he and I walked the same road, but each of us was going in a different direction. "You've got it all figured out, haven't you?"

"I have. And one day, I'll show the world. And they'll never forget me."

Ty, showing the world.

And now the school is his battleground.

No.

My step falters at the thought. Fear reaches out to strangle me as gravity pulls me down.

Strong hands wrap themselves around my elbow, and Chris hoists me to my feet. I gasp for breath.

"Don't think. Don't feel. Just run." Chris's fingers twine through mine.

I nod, feeling infinitely small. If I had breath left to speak, I would whisper a prayer to anyone who might listen.

After twenty-odd paces, my breathing steadies, but my pacing slows. My legs burn. After double the distance, I want to pull my hand away, but his hand squeezes mine. I squeeze back. We might not be able to beat this together, but we definitely can't face it alone.

....

TOMÁS

Fareed walks back into the principal's office to open the windows. I sneak into the hallway and check the area. The long corridors are deserted; the doors to the counselor's office and the resource office are locked. Off the administrative wing are the doors to the quad, to freedom and safety. The main hallway leads deeper into the building, to the classrooms and the auditorium.

The shooting has stopped. It's silent, and that terrifies me.

We can't leave.

The emergency dispatcher's advice is the only advice we have, but a strange sense of calm comes over me. Unless there's a second shooter, everyone's at the other end of the school, which means that for now, we're free to walk around.

Fareed walks up behind me. "You're getting predictable in your old age," he comments. His natural accent has returned. We don't have to pretend around each other. "Someone tells you not to do something, figures you want to do it."

"Did you open the window?" I counter.

"Both of them."

I nod.

"We should open the front doors too," Fareed says.

"We can't leave."

Fareed doesn't immediately reply, and I falter. "Sylvia is in the auditorium. I have to help her. I can't sit back and wait. Not again."

He catches my arm and forces me to look at him. For the scrawniest senior in the history of Opportunity, Far's surprisingly strong—and surprisingly determined. I've never seen this side of him. "If no one else is around, the doors of the auditorium must be locked, and we don't know if the shooter's inside or out. If you're set on going there, we'd better be prepared."

I raise my eyebrows.

"Neil, the janitor," he says. "We can get screwdrivers and hammers from his office. I believe you're more comfortable with tools than with paperwork?"

I put my hand on my chest and feign shock. "You hurt me, my dear fellow. Such mundane activities are far below a man of my standing."

In any other situation, Fareed would have rolled his eyes. In any other situation, I would've grinned at his indignation. Today, all jokes fall flat, though we keep trying. I stuff my hands in my pockets, tense all over. "Good call."

"Yeah." He copies my gesture and legs it toward the south entrance.

We stay close to the walls, pausing at every corner. When the next shot sounds, the echo is duller.

I shiver. "Who would do something like this?"

Fareed stares at me, his face grim. "Let's worry about that after we figure out how to deal with this," he says softly. There is a stoicism about him but also a deep sadness. Has he lost relatives to war? I never thought to ask.

Another thought strikes me. "Far, when's the last time you were at one of Trenton's speeches? If I remember correctly, Neil doesn't go to those things. He might be able to help us himself."

Fareed doesn't slow his pace. "Yeah, maybe."

We turn the last corner.

The janitor's office fits snugly between the main entrance and the gym. Through the windows of the double doors, we can see slate skies overhead. It makes me long to be outside, to breathe the air. But the doors have been locked with heavy chains. There's nowhere we can go.

The door to the janitor's office stands ajar.

....

AUTUMN

"I liked it here once. Opportunity High. Opportunity. It sounds so hopeful."

Ty's spite makes me feel like throwing up my meager breakfast. This morning, I felt so relieved that he was nowhere to be seen, even though I dreaded going to school alone, especially today of all days. But it was better than facing his unpredictable moods. My only focus has been to get into Juilliard early and get through one last semester before both Sylv and I leave Opportunity behind.

It feels like I made those plans an eternity ago.

I pull Sylv to the farthest door. It's not easy to move

through the throng of students. I hesitate, torn between making sure she's all right and making sure we can run if we need to. There'll be no escape if we get caught in the crowd.

I would reach over to push one of Sylv's long curls out of her eyes, but her hands clamp around mine, and I don't think she'll let go anytime soon.

I don't want her to let go.

"I wanted to fit in here." His voice rises and falls with a singsong cadence. He has the gun in one hand. His other rests on his waistband, where, strapped over his dress shirt and slacks, he carries extra magazines, perhaps even another gun. "Instead, I lost everything."

Dad always used to tell me, *He has a hunter's grace, that boy, and the instincts and speed to match it*. Somehow, I don't think this is what he intended.

The masses part in front of Ty. With every step he takes, the students around him scatter from the aisle, down the rows of seats, pushing themselves toward the sides of the room—anything to increase the distance between them and Tyler. Together we could be so strong, but the gun has made us individuals.

"All of you with your perfect lives. Do you know what losing feels like? Do you care?"

When he reaches the front row, Ty veers away from the aisle and climbs the steps onto the stage. His eyes remain ever watchful, scanning his audience. How many of us have hurt him?

From the wings, Mr. Jameson and three other teachers creep toward Ty's side of the stage. Are they going to try to circle him? I suck in a breath. They're underestimating him. Everyone always does.

Our English teacher's hands are stained with Principal Trenton's blood. And I don't know what Ty wants, but if they try to stop him, this'll only get worse.

Suddenly, Ty shifts his attention to the handful of people onstage. "If you cooperate, some of you might go home today. All you have to do is listen carefully to what I'm saying. No screaming, no running, no phones, and certainly no attempting to disarm me. Today, you'll all listen."

To: Sis

HELP ME WE'RE TRAPPED

To: Sis

Claire I'm so scared. He's shooting people.

What do I do. CLAIRE PLEASE PICK UP

CHAPTER SEVEN

SYLV

Hometown, family, God, country: that's the Opportunity creed. It's preached by the mayor who can trace his lineage back to the Civil War and the elderly farmers, like Abuelo, who linger outside church to discuss the crops and the weather. It's what makes our community strong, gives us purpose. Even with my ticket out, this is home, and I don't want to leave.

The Browne family had been part of Opportunity for generations—but no more. When Mrs. Browne died, Ty raged against everyone who tried to help him. He wouldn't eat the food anyone brought; he snarled at our sympathy. Still, the town forgave his grief. Until Mr. Browne drowned his sorrows in alcohol and Tyler doused his in hatred. And after a while, Opportunity took the withdrawal and the lashing out personally. The town stopped trying to bring them back into the fold.

And we lost them.

Autumn was the only one who didn't notice, and if she did, she didn't care. Now her eyes are fixed on Tyler. She's pale, but her eyes are fierce. She is so much stronger than people expect. She is not afraid. Not anymore. Not like I have been for months now.

The only time she saw the same Tyler I did was when we spent the first night of summer together and I told her Tyler found out about us at junior prom.

"Do you think Ty hates us?" she asked.

"He could never hate you."

She plucked aimlessly at a dandelion in the grass. Her face was drawn. "He's been so angry. He doesn't seem to care about anything anymore."

It was the first time she acknowledged her brother wasn't as perfect as she made him out to be and the last time we talked about it. When I leaned against her, she winced and turned away from me.

"What's wrong?"

She tugged her shirt back in place but not before I saw the bruises that spread across her shoulder.

"I fell against one of the wooden posts in the shed. My arm's still sore."

"Autumn…"

"Nothing's wrong." She crushed the flower between her fingers and looked straight at me, as if challenging me to object.

Pity made me bite my tongue. She danced every spare hour, every moment she could get away from Mr. Browne, and she looked pale and wary. Ty was the only family she had left. Right there and then, I didn't want her to know how much he had changed too.

"Tyler may be angry at the entire rest of the world, but he could never hate you."

Autumn seemed unconvinced. "You don't know him like I do."

It was the truest thing she said that night, as we both lied to each other.

I push my nails into my palm. Opportunity cast out Tyler—and by association, his whole family—but Autumn never noticed. She relished being alone. She didn't want to be bound to anyone, and Opportunity severed her ties for her.

"Get back to your seats. I don't want anyone sneaking up on me." Tyler's voice echoes across the room.

Autumn squeezes my hand tighter. "Shhh," she mutters absently, drawing me closer. "Stay here. Don't let him see you." Most of the students stay where they are, yet Tyler seems unperturbed.

Then he turns back toward the stage, and the next bullet buries itself in the leg of one of the approaching teachers. She falls to the stage with a grunt.

"Get down," he says. "Get off the stage."

Mr. Jameson freezes, but neither he nor the other teachers move.

Tyler fires another shot—this time at the remaining chorus members on the stage. They shriek. The teachers back away, toward the front row.

The teachers will be effectively trapped there, but given the choice between life and someone else's death, I wouldn't hesitate either.

"I love how attentive you all are now. Did you ever consider listening to me before?"

In a corner, Mrs. Noble, the new freshman history teacher, huddles against the wall. She only started teaching this year. I don't think this is what she had in mind. Her face is blotched; her hair sticks out in all directions.

The last teacher left onstage, Mr. Jameson stands tall. He must be as terrified as the rest of us, but what strikes me most isn't the nervous tremor in his hands or the patches of sweat on his shirt. It's the genuine pain on his face.

He keeps lifting his hands as if to reach out to Tyler, as he has with every student in each of his classes. He would have listened.

We all hate to love Opportunity High and love to hate it. We can't wait to graduate, but we don't want to leave. This school is special—from the stupid bright-red bricks that make the building look modern and out of place to our school mascot: the Ocelot of Opportunity.

But it's Mr. Jameson who makes this school even more special. Mr. Jameson, who knows the name of every single student in the school, who talks with us all about our dreams and futures, who is a better college counselor than our actual college counselor.

Every year at the start of the spring semester, he builds a bonfire for the seniors in the field on the side of the school. It's tradition, and everyone gathers at midnight for him to read to us. A legend. A short story. A myth. After everyone's eaten themselves sick on marshmallows, he asks students to write their wishes on sky lanterns. And the wishes will be sent up to the stars — and whatever greater power we might believe in. Together, each class dreams about something bigger than this world we live in.

It sounds corny as hell, but every year, all the seniors love it. Even Mr. Jameson's daughter, Mei — who demonstratively avoided her father's classes until graduation — raved about it last year. Because no matter who we are, we all dream. The ritual made Mr. Jameson a legend and Opportunity High our home.

"Mr. Browne, surely that's not..." Mr. Jameson starts.

A ripple of murmurs goes through the auditorium.

Please be silent.

....

TOMÁS

Far skids past me toward the double doors and tries to open them. The locks jingle against the fortified glass, and the sound echoes off the walls. A shiver of claustrophobia creeps up my spine, which is entirely unhelpful.

"C'mon," I say a little too loudly. "We don't know if there are other people outside the auditorium."

Probably not. Most likely not. But we shouldn't risk it.

With the toe of my shoe, I open the janitor's door and peer in. Neil is the only one fortunate enough to be exempt from Trenton's speeches. He wouldn't have been in the auditorium. But there's no sign of him. *Did he go to the auditorium or to get help?*

I flick on the light switch. The fluorescent lamp bathes the room in an unnatural glow.

And I falter.

Neil *is* here. I don't know what I was expecting. Maybe Neil tied to his chair, a rag stuffed in his mouth like you'd see in the movies, his eyes wild and his forehead sweaty from struggling against his bonds. He'd be furious but grateful when we cut through his restraints.

Instead, he sits, leaning against one of his closets. His hands are bound together with a cable tie pulled so tight his fingers have gone black. Cable ties circle his neck, and he is gagged. His eyes are empty; his face is as discolored as his hands. Bloody scratches mark his neck, as if he tried to rip through the plastic with his bare hands.

My ears ring and my stomach revolts. I reach for the garbage can, where I puke until there's not a scrap of food left in my body.

It doesn't make me feel any better.

"Oh my God." Fareed backs away against the wall. He mutters something, but I can't make out the words. It sounds like a prayer of sorts in the language of his parents.

I should probably pray too. Granddad would expect me to. But the sight of Neil's body has made me numb all over.

I have to get to Sylvia. I have to get to the auditorium. I wipe my mouth on my sleeve. "Get me the flag on that shelf," I tell Fareed in a voice I barely recognize as my own. It seems we're both alternate versions of ourselves. I push Neil's eyelids down so he isn't staring anymore. His skin feels like wax, and part of me refuses to believe it's really him, refuses to believe this is really happening. The rest of me demands action—right now.

Fareed hands me the flag—Opportunity's blue-and-crimson school logo, with the school motto in cursive underneath it. Together we drape it over Neil's body so "Future" covers his face.

"The shooter will either be just outside the auditorium

or inside. We need whatever tools we can find for the locks," I manage. "Cutters, crowbars, screwdrivers, pliers, wrenches—whatever Neil's got. Hell, hammers too. If nothing else, we can use them to smash the windows to signal the police or to get out."

Without waiting for me to finish speaking, Fareed climbs on top of the janitor's desk to take down the toolboxes and the first aid kit from the one of the shelves.

I pull open a drawer and start looking for other materials. I somehow doubt Neil will have a set of lock picks or a skeleton key, but paper clips will do just as nicely.

Or a gun.

This isn't about returning fire or self-defense. This is about revenge. If this guy hurt my sister or anyone else, I'll kill him. Slowly.

Except we have school policies against having guns—for students and for staff. Even if Neil had one—in case of emergency—it would've been locked away in a secure location, and finding it, let alone accessing it, would take time we don't have.

I stuff a handful of paper clips into my pocket and accept a bolt cutter and a collection of other tools from Fareed. We'll have to do what we can and pray the police get here fast.

....

CLAIRE

Today is a nightmare. Any moment now I'll wake up.

If it weren't for Jonah, I could convince myself we imagined this. I could convince myself we didn't hear gunshots but a microphone falling or a speaker short-circuiting. Tomorrow, we'd laugh at how we called the police and the National Guard over a technical malfunction. Trace would think it the world's best joke.

Except I know what a gunshot sounds like. I know the difference between a microphone and a starting gun and a semiautomatic. I've seen death.

I know this is real.

"I'll show the world. And they'll never forget me."

The air burns in my lungs. The road stretches out in front of Chris and me, but it feels like we aren't getting any closer to where we want to be.

One, two, forward.

Three, four, still to go.

"C'mon, Sarge, keep up."

My eyes sear with tears of anger. "Don't call me that. Don't ever call me that again."

Chris is temporarily dumbstruck. I take advantage of that, the words tumbling out of my mouth before I can stop them. "If this is Ty's doing, how did I not know?

How did I not see him for who he really is? I thought we were always honest with each other."

Chris shakes his head. "How could you have known? Tyler is clever. He would've been careful. You can't blame yourself."

"Ty told me he would make sure the world remembered him. *He told me*, Chris. I could've done something about it. This never should've happened. I could have protected everyone. I should have protected Matt. I. Did. Nothing."

Chris's jaw tenses and his shoulders strain. He takes several deep, hard breaths and slows his pace.

I match his steps.

"Did Tyler ever tell you he planned to bring a gun to school?" Chris asks finally.

I shake my head.

"When he told you he wanted to get back at the world, was he angry?"

"After his mom died, Ty was always angry." I add, "But he was never angry at me. He was always good to me. He listened, comforted, planned for our future." Ty always tried to find solutions. When I'd had a bad day and just wanted to break something, Ty would hold me and tell me things would get better. I trusted him, even if he never trusted his own reassurances. "But yeah, he'd been in another pointless fight with Tomás and Fareed. Don't make my excuses for me, Chris."

"I'm not." For a step or two, he's silent, his breathing labored. "You know, I always imagined we'd run our last race together. Like our first race. Do you remember that? I'd forgotten my running shoes, but instead of borrowing a pair for tryouts, I figured winning all my races in middle school entitled me to a place on the team. We were both convinced we were amazing runners. I still don't know what Coach saw in us."

"At least I brought the right shoes," I protest flatly.

The corner of Chris's mouth quirks up. "You were ten minutes late."

That was the day Trace enlisted. She called to tell me, and I locked myself in a bathroom stall to talk her through her nerves.

"That was the first time I lost a race. Every other time, I lost on purpose. Not because you weren't good enough to beat me but because you are. You are so much better than me, and some days, running is all I have. If I lose, I want it to be on my terms. But knowing you were near me kept me going." He hesitates. "You can live up to *anyone*."

I turn to stare at Chris, but he's focused on the road ahead. The stammer of my heart has nothing to do with fear now.

"I always thought you were generous, that you let me win to make me feel better." That was what made us the best of friends from the start, ever since that very first day. If Ty hadn't paired up with me in English, if he hadn't asked me out first, perhaps I would've figured out if Chris meant something more. But I never thought he wanted to be more than just friends.

Chris's fingers brush mine. "I never thought you needed to win to be perfect."

....

AUTUMN

The entire auditorium is fixated on the two people onstage. The rows of seats at the front of the auditorium are empty, except for a handful of teachers. Everyone has found a way to move away from Tyler. He stands in the spotlight at the center of our universe.

And I—I should be more afraid.

But I refuse.

"Mr. Browne..." Mr. Jameson tries again. He takes a hesitant step forward.

"LISTEN." Ty swings the gun to the side. A loud shot reclaims the silence. From here, I can't see if he's hit anyone. I don't even know if he knows, let alone cares. "The time for talking has passed. Move." He waits for Mr. Jameson to comply and then continues firmly, "Now."

Mr. Jameson looks gray, and there are dark patches of sweat on his shirt. He nods but lingers on the steps.

Ty's finger eases off the trigger, and his shoulders relax. "Now then. Good. This shouldn't be too complicated." Tyler stands with his back to the far wall so no one can sneak up on him. "To survive, you must know who your friends are. You must know who you can trust. And you must know how to stop caring."

The auditorium is still, everyone too scared to speak. People huddle together, arms wrapped around shoulders, fingers entangled.

Ty flashes a comfortable smile—a smile I'd seen only a couple nights ago when he dangled my ballet shoes in front of Dad, let it slip I was still dancing. His smile was just like Dad's—cold. And Ty stood by while Dad showed me that the love he once had for dance, for me, died along with Mom.

I rub the back of my neck and try to ease the tension. Yesterday, Ty swore it was an accident. He laughed through his tears. We need each other, he said, because we had no one else. When he tended my bruises, he told me he'd take care of me, told me he'd forge a doctor's note because it'd be better for me to stay home. He promised there was nothing that made him happier than to see me dance. It reminded him of when Mom was alive and we'd go see her performances. He said that even though he'd never felt the extremes of Dad's anger, he'd already lost so much. We both had.

I believed him. I wanted to believe him. He's my brother.

"Where are my former classmates? Raise your hands." Ty's voice drops, and it makes the hair on my neck stand up straight. A few people tentatively raise their hands. Most stay crouched down. It feels like inviting death to speak up, but Ty is all seriousness. His eyes narrow, and his next shot makes me jump.

Bang.

"You cowards. HANDS."

More seniors raise their hands. I squeeze Sylv's tighter to make sure she doesn't.

"Much better." It's like this is some messed-up game of Simon Says, and perhaps it is to Ty. After all, with one simple question, he's located most of the senior class.

Everyone he despises.

Letting the gun dangle by his side, he takes a few casual steps toward the edge of the stage.

"Did you miss me? I always wondered what made you decide I wasn't good enough. No matter."

He turns on his heel and raises the gun in one fluid motion. Without a second glance, without so much as a blink, he pulls the trigger and shoots Mr. Jameson. The

88

first bullet buries itself in the teacher's arm. The second bullet drills a hole through his chest. "Lesson one: don't get attached and you won't get hurt."

No one moves. We're all in shock. My hands are shaking, though I desperately try to keep calm.

"Be smart. Don't get in the way of the guy with the gun."

The barrel of the gun arcs toward the audience again, pointing at a student crouching between the rows of seats. I can see it's Jordan, one of Sylv's friends and her lab partner in AP Chemistry. Jordan, who always wears the geekiest T-shirts but is secretly a baseball fan.

Jordan, who helped take care of Sylv's mother after she fell ill, who wants to become a doctor, who's going to be premed next year.

Jordan, who didn't raise his hand.

"Lesson two: follow the instructions." Tyler crouches and aims carefully. Then he pulls the trigger.

"Bang, bang, you're dead."

Jay Eyck
@JEyck32

OMG #OHS

10:13 AM

74 retweets

Jay Eyck
@JEyck32

Nonononoo. This cant be real. Anyone at #OHS?!

10:14 AM

Anonymous
@BoredOpportunist

@JEyck32 Hahaha dude keep up. Are you still drunk?

10:14 AM

Jay (@JEyck32) ➜ Kevin (@KeviiinDR)

Pls answer me. Pls tell me you're okay.

10:15 AM

CHAPTER EIGHT

TOMÁS

More shots mar the silence, and all I want to do is barge into the auditorium. If screwdrivers and paper clips are all I have, screwdrivers and paper clips are what I'll use. It's better than not doing anything.

"Do we need to open these doors first?" Fareed hesitates outside the janitor's office, staring at the main entrance, our gateway to freedom. His question stops me in my tracks. We need an emergency exit. But getting these doors open means precious time away from the auditorium.

"We can smash the windows?" he thinks out loud. "Then people could crawl out. Or we can try to cut through the chains."

I glance at the bolt cutter in my hands, then toss it to him. He barely manages to catch it.

"Cut the chains if you can," I say. "Once you're done, get to the main entrance. Open as many doors as you can and then come find me."

Fareed nods.

"If the police get here before you're through, make sure they don't mistake the cutter for a weapon," I say. "Just in case."

He grimaces. "Run like the wind. You have damsels in distress to rescue and people to save."

For a second, we both stand motionless and stare at each other. We want our words to sound like jokes, but with the broken look Fareed gives me, they're anything but.

I salute him with one of the screwdrivers before I take off running through the empty halls. At every corner, I expect to turn and find students streaming through the halls, to hear the slams of opening and closing lockers. I close my eyes, and I can see and hear my peers all around me. Just another day of class.

My feet go so fast. I fly through the halls. But the closer I get to the auditorium, the louder my heart beats. I listen to the silence and wait for the inevitable sound of gunshots.

I slow and inch toward the corner, staring down the next hall.

No one.

Three empty hallways converge in front of the auditorium doors. It's the very core of Opportunity High. Lockers line the walls, the blue doors repainted over winter break. It looks as though they're unused, as if everything about this school is new and surreal.

Stairwells lead up to the study rooms and science classrooms and, beyond those, the roof.

Five sets of doors lead to the auditorium. Four of the double doors are chained and secured with padlocks. The one to the far right isn't. It makes me realize how vulnerable the auditorium is. With these doors locked, only the emergency exits and the entryway to the wings remain, and none of those lead directly outside. If the shooter was prepared for these doors, they were probably prepared for any other options as well. It means the auditorium is virtually inaccessible, the perfect place to trap all students.

I move slowly, but my sneakers squeak on the freshly waxed linoleum. I pass the unchained door in favor of the one on the far left. It may be locked from the inside, and unless whoever's got the gun has moved, it seems safer to start at the far end. It seems better not to make any assumptions. Better to focus on the locks in front of me.

Focus and not listen.

Impossible.

I push the screwdrivers into my belt so none will fall out, and I edge toward the door. There's no sound on the other side. The auditorium was built for music performances as well as drum band practice and is practically soundproof.

When someone on the other side of the door speaks, it sounds like faint mumbling. Distant. Unintelligible.

I dig out two paper clips and bend them into straight

paper clips, then kneel down next to the door. With one hand, I hold the lock steady, and with the other, I slowly insert the paper clips. If Principal Trenton could see me now, she'd have a thing or two to say. *No breaking into student files; no breaking into school property.*

I shiver. I would promise her to never break any rules, ever again, if only it would mean my sister is safe.

....

SYLV

My brothers may think I'm the strong one, but here — next to Autumn, whose watchful eyes scan the room — I know it's not true. I know how to care for others. I know how to talk to Mamá when she forgets the world around her, but I'm not strong. For the first time in months, I want someone to hold me. If only Tomás were here. Or Abuelo. Anyone who could make sense of this madness.

Anyone who could protect us.

Because I can't ask Autumn to stand up against her brother. I can only try to take care of myself, like I've always done.

Ah, Dios, if only Tomás's detention has kept him safe. Of all the days to come to school instead of skip, I wish he hadn't chosen today. We only just started talking again.

With my back against the wall, I'm so close to the

doors—to freedom—but with the doors locked, we might as well be behind iron bars.

Onstage, Tyler rights himself from his crouching position. "I'm thirsty. Does anyone have a drink?"

I choke on a hysterical giggle, and the incredulousness ripples around me. No one speaks, although there are rustles as people reach toward their bags. We all understand the value of following instructions, but no one steps forward.

"No one?" Tyler taps his chin with the gun. "Bottled water? A can of soda? *Nothing*?"

No one moves. Tyler has the entire auditorium bound to him.

"You there." Tyler gestures at a boy in the aisle with whom we've shared years of classes. It's Kevin Rolland, one of Opportunity High School's only out-and-proud students. He was kind to everyone. He once climbed on his desk in history class during a debate with Tyler, when Tyler argued that outsiders like Kevin had no place in Opportunity, that Opportunity should protect its own.

But every time Tyler tried to speak, Kevin spoke louder, reciting half of Harvey Milk's "Hope for a better tomorrow" speech before the teacher asked him to step down. Most of the class applauded, not necessarily because they agreed with Kevin but because he'd stood up to Tyler's bullying. During lunch that day, one of Kevin's friends, Jay, "accidentally" tipped his soda on Tyler, drenching his clothes. When Kevin found his tires slashed at the end of the day, someone set fire to Ty's locker in retaliation.

And it kept escalating until Tyler dropped out. It was almost the end of the year anyway, and we were all glad to see him go.

"I'm *thirsty*, Kevin," Tyler says.

Kevin rummages in his bag. His face is bright red when he looks up and mouths, "Nothing." It seems fear has stolen his voice, like it has stolen so many of ours.

"Shame."

I barely have time to look away before another shot shatters the morning, and Kevin tumbles back.

"All I ever asked for was a chance. A chance like you gave him or her." He carefully punctuates his words. He squints and aims at one of the juniors. Fires.

If he'd gone on a murdering spree, it would've been less scary. It would've been a random act of violence. The simple fact that he carefully picks out his targets, among the hundreds of students in the auditorium, makes him far more of a threat. And it terrifies me.

Tyler will shoot everyone who tries to stop him, who gets in his way, but they're collateral damage. They're not who he came here for.

We are. Those of us who do not fit into his perfect world.

I glance at Autumn. Tyler would do anything for her, and she would do anything for Tyler. Or at least, she would have. Now she is a statue, as frightened as the rest of us. Beneath her bouncy blond hair and her light makeup, she's pasty white. And I want to wrap my arms around her, no matter who sees. Because what's left to be afraid of when our worst fear is already here?

The three freshman girls next to us sob. They keep their heads down and their arms around each other's shoulders so they don't have to face the horror.

I wish I had the courage to stand up to Tyler.

When I push myself to my knees, a shadow catches my eye. There's a thin ray of light coming from under the heavy doors, and there's a subtle difference in the shadow, like someone's out there. One of Tyler's accomplices? Does he even *have* accomplices? Did he ever have friends?

I inch closer, but then Tyler speaks again, and I freeze in my tracks. "Today, all of you belong to me."

The outside world no longer matters.

....

CLAIRE

"I've always thought you were perfect, and if I hated Tyler, it was because he made you believe what I've known for such a long time. You took command this morning when none of us could. You're good in crises. You're clever. You're strong. And you can't blame yourself for what's happening today, because if you go down that road, you'll never be able to turn back. You did the best you could."

Chris's kindness thaws my fear, but I know being forgiven is not as easy as that. Not when he only knows half the story and I'm still connecting the dots. I want to reach out to him, but this is not the time. We need to keep moving.

I slow my pacing to get a little more oxygen. *Bad idea.* It feels like inhaling ice. My heart may burst. Every race I've ever run has a moment when I want to give up. When the pain becomes too much and my legs feel like lead. Coach always told us, if you can get through that moment, you've beaten half your opponents.

I focus on the horizon and on the silhouette of Opportunity. The old clock tower and the church. The grain silos, which, according to Matt, look like castle battlements. The skyline isn't impressive, but it's familiar. It's home.

"Ty wasn't just angry," I manage at last. "He was vindictive. When he got into fights with Tomás, he wouldn't take it out on him. He'd take it out on the people close to you. He cornered Tomás's sister during junior prom and tried to kiss her. That was why we broke up that night. Ty told me later he only meant it as a joke."

JROTC was at prom as honor guard, and I was making my rounds when I heard someone cry out.

"You need to learn some manners," he hissed at her.

She tried to maneuver out from under his arms. "Fuck off, Tyler. I'm not interested in you."

He leaned closer. "I'll teach you."

"He assaulted her as a joke, a warning, and I only told him to get lost. Sylv didn't want me to report it, so I never did, but I should've done more."

That night, Ty stared at me with a wildness in his eyes that I'd never seen before. Gone were kindness and patience. Gone were the smiles. What was left was feral.

I dragged him away from Sylvia before I turned on him, and it was all I could do to keep from screaming.

"What the hell, Ty? What is wrong with you?"

He flinched, and Sylvia took her chance to run back inside. If I thought her disappearance would calm Ty, I was mistaken. He was seething. "Why is it always about me? This town—this school is taking everything away from me. My home. My mother. My sister. Why am I to blame?"

"So this is what, revenge?"

"I didn't mean anything by it!"

"Sylvia has nothing to do with your fights with Tomás. I have nothing to do with your fights with Tomás." I fought to keep my emotions under control, but all I wanted was to pound on him. Or cry. Or both. "I thought you cared about me."

Something like terror flashed across his face. "I do. Of course I do."

He stepped closer to me.

I shook my head and pulled back. "You are disgusting. Leave me alone."

His jaw tensed. I expected him to lash out at me. But then his shoulders sagged. "You can't... Please don't leave me too."

I sighed. "Go home, Ty."

The next day, he dropped out.

When I saw him at the Browne hardware store a week or so later, he smiled and asked about Matt and Trace. We were both a little awkward and reserved, but I thought he only temporarily lost control, like on days when the grief over his mother overwhelmed him. But he never apologized. And neither did I.

Chris picks up the pace until we're running again and gravity itself releases us—until every step takes us farther away from the pain.

"We're more than our mistakes. We're more than what people expect of us. I have to believe that." Chris's breathing is a little a deeper, but that's the only sign he's pushing himself. "You can do far more than you ever imagined. If you don't believe that, at least believe me."

"Yes, Commander." I can't smile, but his words make my steps a little lighter. "I don't know what to do when you're not by my side."

"Are we okay?"

I sigh. "Of course we are. You're my best friend. Nothing will ever change that."

He stares at me as if he's not sure anymore.

Our footsteps sound on the concrete, one in front of the other in front of the other. In the distance, sirens pierce the air.

I squeeze his hand, and he squeezes mine in return.

Then the road drops away, and I can't breathe anymore, and I'm falling, falling, falling.

....

AUTUMN

Sylv backs against the door. I trail her finger with my thumbnail. She's had so much going on with her family; she's been so strong. I can't stand the idea that after all she's been through, my brother's actions are what breaks her. I scour my mind for comforting words: "Just hold on"? "We'll get out of here"? No. They're all empty promises. "Ty knows what he's doing."

She shivers. "Then what do *we* do?"

With the hundreds of cell phones in the auditorium, someone must have alerted the authorities. "We keep our heads down and hope he doesn't see us," I say. "We follow instructions."

This auditorium is our world now, and we're all slowly

dying. Ty casually changes magazines. He tosses the used one on the floor like a crumpled ball of paper.

"Do you know what it feels like to lose everything you hold dear? Your family? Your girlfriend? For your *entire town* to turn against you too? Arrogant Tyler. Idiotic Tyler. Outcast Tyler. I'm reclaiming Opportunity. Your *lives* are mine. And you will pay attention."

Where did he even get the gun? One of the trade shows Dad used to attend? I can see them now, laughing together like they never laughed with me, Dad commenting on the quality of the weapon, or the right ammunition, or the best way to clean the barrel.

My head feels light, as if I did a thousand pirouettes. The back of my throat burns. I don't want this pain. We can never undo this.

I want to go back to when Ty took care of me like a big brother. To go back to a time before we fell apart. To stop this from ever happening. I want to slap some sense into him, tell him to think about everything he's losing now, but I'm frozen. If he wants revenge, he should take it out on me.

Releasing Sylv, I stay low to the ground and crawl to get a better look at the stage. I never thought this was how I'd apply my dance techniques, but I move quietly and swiftly. If Ty finds me, at least Sylv will still be hidden in the back of the auditorium with a hundred other students.

Ty's voice shakes the auditorium, and my heart sinks when he stops to focus on another student. The people around me sit, crouch, hunch. They barely move as I try to get past. I keep my head down and crawl. I weave between their legs and around their bodies until I'm staring at the steps to the stage, protected by of a row of seats.

In time to see the next shot. I rest my cheek against the rough carpeting and close my eyes.

He sat on my bed on Christmas Eve, playing with the Juilliard audition invitation. "You should be more careful, lil Sis," he said. "Dad will kill you if he sees this."

"Give it back."

I snatched at it, but he kept it out of reach. "Don't worry. I've always kept your secrets."

I raised my eyebrows. Over the last few months, after Claire broke up with him and he dropped out, Ty lost interest in my secrets, the future, our family, me. He helped Dad in his shop during the week and disappeared on weekends to hunt. He got Dad's grudging respect, while I got left behind.

I missed my brother.

"You should get out of here. Away from your so-called girlfriend. Show Opportunity it is too small for your talent. We'll show them no one messes with the Brownes."

I reached for Julliard's letter again, and this time he let me grab it.

"What do you want, Ty?"

He pushed a stray strand of hair out of his face and shrugged. "There's nothing keeping you here. Not her. Not Dad. Not me." The corner of his mouth twitched. That was his tell. He was bluffing. He could never play poker for money.

But I couldn't tell him the truth. I couldn't give him hope.

I stuffed the letter into my pocket. "No. There isn't. And the sooner I can get out, the better. Get lost, Ty."

His face twisted into a grimace, but he didn't say another word.

"Shall I let you in on something?" Tapping the barrel of the gun against his chin, Ty raises an eyebrow and his voice softens. "I thought my family at least cared about me. But you corrupted them. You left nothing for me." He fires another bullet into the audience, and this time there is a cry of pain. It seems to calm him a little.

"Wouldn't you agree, Autumn?" He pans the audience, waiting for me to come forward. Waiting for me to surrender.

CJ Johnson
@CadetCJJ

I always thought I'd be braver but I'm so afraid. I'm so afraid. #OHS

10:17 AM

74 favorites

George Johnson
@G_Johnson1

@CadetCJJ THINKING OF YOU COZ. PLS TAKE CARE.

10:17 AM

Abby Smith
@YetAnotherASmith

@CadetCJJ @G_Johnson1 We all are.

10:17 AM

Family North
@FamNorthOpp

@YetAnotherASmith @CadetCJJ @G_Johnson1 All thinking of you.

10:18 AM

Jim Tomason

@JTomasonSTAR

@CadetCJJ Can we ask you some questions about the situation at #OHS? Our reporters would like to get in touch.

10:18 AM

CHAPTER NINE

AUTUMN

No one reacts. The people around me shift uncomfortably, but they don't speak up, point, or do anything that might betray my presence. And that surprises me. Few people here like me, and my brother is threatening them with death. Sacrificing me could be their ticket out of this hellhole.

"Autumn," Ty singsongs. "Would it help if I gave you an incentive to make the right decision?"

He jumps off the stage and paces in front of the students like he's deciding who to pick for his basketball team in PE. Miles, who spent all of junior year teasing Ty about his suits? Eve, who had a crush on Ty sophomore year but dumped him for Miles? They're sitting next to each other. Their hands squeezed together so hard they've turned white.

Ty stops in front of them. He taps the barrel of his gun against his chin again. Eve hides her face in Miles's shoulder. Waves of tension roll off of them. The stares from the people around me burn.

Last year, on the first anniversary of Mom's death, Ty woke me up at the break of dawn. Dad was still asleep, the whole house smelling like beer.

Ty smiled at me. "Let's play hooky."

Technically, we had no obligations to escape—on Sundays, the store was closed. But the alternative was spending the day with Dad, and he would be hungover and unpredictable. Tyler's three words loosened the noose of fear around my heart.

Tyler drove us to the cemetery; then we got fries at the diner and he took me to a fringe performance of the Tuscaloosa dance company. It was a modern retelling of Othello. The performance wasn't particularly good— half the dancers weren't classically trained and the music was courtesy of an ancient record player—but it was the first performance I'd seen since Mom died. The first time I felt safe.

It was perfect.

I hoped Ty's return to Opportunity High meant I'd get my brother back. I didn't want to be alone today. But not like this. Never like this.

I swallow. This is no time for emotions.

Ty grins, shoots Miles, and moves on. Eve screams again and again, but Ty ignores her. A few steps farther, he leans over the seats and pulls up a black girl by her baseball jersey.

"NYAH!" The strangled cry comes from close by. My heart stops. It won't start beating again.

In the aisle, Asha tries to get up while three others pull her down. But Asha is fierce. She stands.

My eyes burn. I should get up. I should stop this.

Oh, Ty.

"Ash, help me!" The girl struggles in Ty's grip, but he's too strong and none too gentle when he drags her over the row of seats. She's young—a sophomore maybe. Her hair's escaped from her braid, and her shoulders shake.

I should leap to my feet, but my arms and legs are leaden. I can't move.

"It's a terrifying idea, isn't it? Losing everything you care about?" Ty asks calmly as he aims the gun at the girl. "I don't *want* to do this, Autumn."

"No, no, no. Please don't. Oh my God, please don't." The girl's sobs fills the auditorium. She's the first one to beg. The first one to stare into the barrel of the gun as he taunts her. The first one to break. "Help me. Someone, help me!"

She sounds so young. Too young to die. Like all the rest of us, she's supposed to have a future. She's supposed to study hard and coast through high school. Make mistakes, make friends. Screw up, screw boys. Instead, she's reduced to an example, a statistic. And I know the auditorium may be big enough to hold a thousand students, but it's too small to hide just one.

....

TOMÁS

Years ago, Granddad set out to teach my brothers and me the tricks of running a farm—mucking stables, repairing tools, and one day, the finer art of lock work. He didn't think picking locks was appropriate for a girl, so Sylvia got left behind and it was just the four of us. A men's day out.

Sylv didn't like it one bit. She was a sight: an eight-year-old in pigtails and flowered pink overalls stomping through the fields, trying to follow and spy on us. Granddad doted on her but he put his foot down. We watched as he crouched in front of her and explained that she didn't have to understand farm life. She had a bright future ahead of her. She was his *mariposa,* his butterfly, and the apple of his eye.

She huffed and puffed about it up in her tree house for days.

Sylvia, my opposite, who cares for Mamá as easy as Granddad does. Who cared for Gran and humored her belief in spirits and brujería as causes for Mamá's forgetfulness and Gran's pains and aches.

She never convinced Granddad to teach her how to pick locks, but she joined us fishing and hunting every chance she got before Mamá got sick. She loved the hard work.

Sylv used to be fierce and fearless.

And even when she fell ill last summer, she still helped out on the farm. With her stellar grades, she could get into every school in the freaking country. She is perfect in every way, and if I didn't love her so much, I would've hated her for setting the bar impossibly high.

When I told Granddad I wanted to go to college too, he just patted my shoulder and told me the farm would always be there for me. He never believed I could do it.

The paper clip twists and snaps. *Hell*.

The flimsy clips are no alternative to lock picks. Abue—Granddad showed us how to pick rusty, old padlocks. The heavy-duty locks that fasten these chains are not the cheap-ass things they sell at the Browne hardware store. Whoever bought these wanted to make sure no one gets out alive.

Hopefully Fareed has better luck on his side of the school. If there's anyone I trust to do this, it's him. He and Sylvia, they are confident.

Fareed is the only Muslim student at Opportunity. He stands out in the crowd, with his easy ways and melodic accent. But he woos the teachers and has them wrapped around his little finger. He keeps the language of his parents. He prays several times a day. He is confident in his traditions.

And I envy it.

Ah, I wish I remembered the words to *Padre Nuestro* or *Ave María*. I wish my abuelo were here, so I could watch him work this lock. My mother doesn't recognize me, and my sister doesn't recognize me. If I don't get out of here, what will be left of me? Who will remember me?

It's easier to know who I'm not than to know who I am. When everyone expects me to fail, it's easier to give up than to try.

The next gunshot makes my knees buckle.

....

SYLV

My heart seizes. *Nyah.* The warning shot passed right by her.

Several feet in front of me, Asha shouts and scrambles toward her little sister.

"Ash, help me!" On the far side of the auditorium, Nyah squirms in Tyler's grip. She's a talented pitcher with a strong arm, but Tyler is stronger. He has the gun. And Nyah can only beg for help. "No, no, no. Please don't. Oh my God, please don't."

My nails scratch at the carpet until my fingertips burn. Then I dart forward.

On my knees, I grasp at Asha's ankles. I'm vaguely aware of other hands pulling at Asha too. She is liable to strike us all down for getting in her way. But even with her determination, she can't part this sea of students.

We pull her to the ground, and I wrap her in a hug while she struggles against me. I don't want to hurt her, but if I can keep her safe—if it's the only thing I do today—it will have meant something.

She will hate me for it. If Tomás were at risk, I would want to protect him. But there is no protection from Tyler. He clearly doesn't care about anything anymore. He hasn't cared about anything since junior prom, when everything started to spin out of control.

Until that night, he stayed aloof, despite spray-painted lockers and messages scratched into the hood of his car. He tricked us with his eloquence and the occasional fake smile. We never saw him for what he really was, and now it is too late.

Down the aisle, Autumn crawls, leaving a wave of unease in her wake. If she hides with our classmates, he won't immediately see her. Maybe that will keep her safe.

"It's easy, Autumn," Tyler continues. "Either you come down here or I continue tormenting your friends.

Oh wait. You don't have friends. Come out or I'll pick off the entire school. Just. Like. This."

The shot mingles with Asha's shriek of grief. But she stops struggling, as if everything worth fighting for has died at that moment.

And a piece of me dies too.

....

CLAIRE

We hear the sirens first, their sound deceptively close. There are no cars in sight. In the far distance, the road seems to shimmer with the heat of engines.

"Claire."

My mouth tastes of blood and metal. I must've bitten my lip when I tripped. I press my face against the concrete, savoring the cold against my cheek. I close my eyes and feel for the vibration of the road.

Above me, Chris looms, tall and dark. He breathes hard, his hands pressed to his sides. "Claire, get up. If you cool down too much, your muscles will seize."

His words sound different, as if they are coming to me through a thick fog.

Flickering blue lights appear on the horizon as the sirens grow closer. Their cry makes me want to cover my ears—it's all too loud.

"Claire, think about Matt."

I snap back. Chris's face swims into clarity above me, a deep frown betraying his concern. He reaches out a hand, and I grab it. Sharp pain shoots through my calves as he pulls me to my feet. Keeping hold of his arm, I lean forward and stretch as far as I can.

The first police car zooms by without stopping.

My stomach revolts, and I retch until I'm gasping for air. Chris's hands gently push my hair out of my face.

"I'm sorry," he says. "I didn't mean to—"

I shake my head. No matter how hard we fight, he's always here for me. And that means everything.

Four, five, six more cars pass us, covering us in dust from the road and fading exhaust fumes.

"You're right," I reply. Matt is my responsibility. I am supposed to protect him, and now I'm not even there for him. "Thank you."

The last car in line screeches to a halt, and a young police officer rolls down her window and leans out.

"Are you OHS kids?" she asks, her voice clipped.

"Yes, ma'am," Chris says.

The officer nods and jerks her head. "Get in. We can't have you wandering around campus today."

When she unlocks the door, a weight lifts off my chest. She'll bring us back to Opportunity High—bring me to Matt. It must be a sign. We can *do* something. This will work out. Everything will work out. Everyone will be okay. *Somehow.*

The officer pauses with a stern frown. "This is not some kind of heroic mission. You'll stay with me until someone can escort you to Opportunity or your homes. Let's go."

"Yes, ma'am," we chorus. Before she can say anything else, I slide into the car and Chris follows me. The smell of leather and rubber tires overwhelms my senses, and it's as familiar as settling into Jonah's car. But the constant radio transmissions talk about threats and shootings. And I'm uneasy instead of comforted.

The Adventures of Mei

Current location: Home

>> Dad won't reply to my texts. There are so many sirens. The cars pass by our home on their way to school, and everything lights up blue. I don't want to know what they'll find. Everyone I know is at OHS.

Comments: <12>

OMG. Is there anything I can do to help? Praying for you.

Have you heard from your dad? Is everything okay?

Such a hoax. You're not even at Opportunity. You just want to get readers.

EWWW. Does that make you feel better? You're disgusting. Why would anyone lie about this? Are you really that narrow-minded? If you have nothing positive to say, why don't you just stay away from this discussion? We wouldn't miss you at all.

CHAPTER TEN

CLAIRE

We're going back, and it's comfort and terror all wrapped into a bundle of emotions. *Matt...*

I can't stop thinking about him—the concentration in his green eyes as he works on his pewter figurines. His grin whenever he challenges Chris to a fight, whenever he chats with Trace. The way he looked up to Ty. The annoyance every time strangers stare at his crutches.

I can't...

I need my mind clear to deal with whatever is waiting for us once we are back at the school. I need to make sure Matt's safe. I want to help our track team, our cadets, everyone.

I place my hand over Chris's.

Without footsteps to count, I listen to the wheels thump over the seams in the uneven road—*one two three, one two three*.

We'll be stronger than our fear. We'll make it out of here today. We'll find a way.

Even this road is proof of that. The Road to Opportunity. It's part of our traditions, our team, our certainties.

Every summer when school's out, the entire track team runs to campus together. Even the field athletes. In the woods behind the parking lot and the football grounds, we'll camp out. Between the school grounds and the tree line, there's a perfect private field.

We'll eat pastries from the local bakery, courtesy of Avery's mother; chocolate, as much as we can carry; popcorn; rock candy; licorice for Chris, though I can't stand the taste.

No alcohol until the JV athletes are asleep, but then we'll drink. We'll toast our four years together, Chris and I, staying up until the break of dawn. It'd be a waste to sleep through our last night as students at Opportunity.

We'll watch the stars fade and the moon disappear. We'll watch the sun set fire to the horizon. And we'll talk about the future one last time before it's actually upon us.

We'll be together.

It'll be the night we'll remember as the best of high school.

We just have to make it there, one day at a time.

....

TOMÁS

The second and third paper clip break under the pressure too. *Snap. Snap.* One after another, I drop them on the linoleum.

I rock back on my heels, stand, and step away to keep from slamming the door in frustration.

I walk back toward the main corridor and glance around the corner. Nothing. No Fareed. No police. Just endless, oppressing silence. Nothing that proves there are a thousand students in the building. They should be in these halls, laughing, arguing, tripping each other.

The heavy doors keep out so many sounds—but I need something to distract me from the noise in my head.

Back at the door, I drop to my knees. I straighten two new paper clips. Insert one into the lock, then the other. Push all other thoughts from my mind.

When I wrench the first tip down, it slips past the pins of the locking mechanism.

I wipe my sweaty fingers on my jeans. I push the second paper clip into the lock and begin exerting pressure again. I should have searched around Neil's office for larger clips because these are too small for a good grip. Still, the first pins give way.

Three pins down.

The paper clip slips over the next.

One more.

A knock echoes through the door, and I jerk back. The padlock swings from my hand, but I manage to grab it before it hits the door.

There's a second knock.

Crap.

The door muffles the sounds inside the auditorium, but how the hell do I know if it's true the other way around? I avoid assemblies if I can, though usually that means missing the bus or skipping school. I have no idea how far the sound of my picking the locks carries. I have no idea what is on the other side of the door. It might be someone trying to get out. It might be a gunman waiting to blast my brains out. I don't know what frightens me more.

I hesitate, then palm a screwdriver like a weapon.

Steeling myself, I crouch so I can run if I need to and raise my hand to rap on the door. Near the corner so the sound won't carry. An unconscious melody.

....

SYLV

Asha feels brittle. We're poised for flight, but there's nowhere to go. Getting out alive is no longer the goal—not dying yet is.

Knocking may have been a disastrous plan, but the

shadows kept moving. I have to know what's out there—who's out there. And between the sobbing and Tyler's proclamations, no one pays attention to me.

My hand still hovers by the door.

My heart rate picks up.

From the other side of the door comes a familiar rhythm. It's the beat of a song Abuelo always hummed for us when we were smaller. For the first time, I dare to hope. Tyler wouldn't have known Tomás spent the morning in detention. He wouldn't have gone looking for him first. Tomás wouldn't be locked in.

He's alive.

He could get us out of here.

The sudden onslaught of hope makes me dizzy. Surreptitiously, I scan the area around me. No one has eyes for anyone but Tyler—and Autumn.

Autumn, who is walking toward her brother.

No… My breath catches. *No, she can't.*

Autumn's face is drawn. She holds herself ramrod straight. With every step she takes, she seems to shrink a little more. I can't remember the last time she laughed without reservation. I can't remember seeing her as happy as she used to be, sitting on a wooden fence with her back to the cotton fields and the sunset, smiling as Mrs. Browne demonstrated a dance pose.

She can't give into him now. He'll never let her go.

He'll never let us go. *She's not the one he wants. His revenge isn't for her.*

But in her position, I would do the same. When Mamá fell ill, my brothers came from all over the country to help us close her law office and move out of our house and to Abuelo's farm. When Tomás almost got kicked out of Opportunity High, Abuelo and I talked to Principal Trenton to prevent that from happening. When I told my family about my girlfriend, they celebrated my happiness even though Father Jones preaches about sin, hell, and damnation.

I would stay in Opportunity and give up my dreams for my family.

I can't imagine what it's like not to have that. For as much as I despise Tyler, I love Autumn. It's why I could never tell her what he did. I want her to be able to keep the only true family she has.

Autumn is breaking away from us all, and there's nothing I can do. I would run to her, cling to her, but at the same time, I want to hug my brother and never let him go. For so many months, we've barely spoken, but his being here gives me strength I didn't know I had. I want to hold on to them both.

I can't lose them.

I finish the song Tomás started.

....

AUTUMN

Every time I blink, I see Nyah's face being torn apart by a bullet. Asha's scream echoes in my ears—or perhaps she's still screaming. Ty is my only brother, but right now, I want him to die. To take the gun and shoot himself.

Or for me to wake up from this nightmare and for everything to go back to normal again.

I keep my eyes staunchly on Ty and try to ignore the people around me. The looks are no longer pitiful, no longer worried about my poor, fucked-up home. Instead it's all anger, fear, hatred. They blame me for Nyah's death, and rightly so. If only I'd spoken up, I might have saved her.

I hope Sylv isn't watching, that she's turned away too.

It proves harder for Ty to get his hands on the kid next to Nyah, who has the common sense to crawl away under the seats. The boy shimmies away, but when a pair of red crutches clatter to the floor, I gasp.

Matt. I never met him, but Ty always spoke fondly of the boy. While I spent long summer evenings with Sylv, Matt and Claire were the family Ty never had.

If Matt isn't safe, none of us are.

I'm torn between my brother, my best friend, my protector, who used to sneak me chocolate after dance practice, the Ty I lost along the way, and this stranger in front of me. When he dug up my hidden ballet shoes to show Dad I never stopped dancing, he stood back and let Dad beat me until I thought Dad was going to kill me. Who is this person I call my brother? I don't even know who we are now. But for what we once were to each other, maybe there is something I can do. If anyone can get through to him, it's me. I have to try.

I stand. No one notices me. All eyes are fixed on Ty and his next victim.

"Tyler." My voice is nothing more than a hoarse whisper. I swallow hard. Numbness trickles down my spine to my fingertips.

Murmurs surround me. Heads turn. The broken silence gives me strength. I clear my throat again before Tyler can shoot another student in my stead.

"Tyler. I'm here."

CJ Johnson
@CadetCJJ
I can't find my brother. My friends are dying.
This is hell. #OHS
10:21 AM

CJ Johnson
@CadetCJJ
He said we ruined his life and now we'll
never escape. #OHS
10:21 AM

Jim Tomason
@JTomasonSTAR
@CadetCJJ Do you feel #OHS is to blame
for the situation? Our reporters would like to
get in touch.
10:22 AM

CHAPTER ELEVEN

TOMÁS

The knocks on the other side of the door complete my song. I knock again. She replies. She. Sylvia. I knew she was in the auditorium, like a good student, but the confirmation kills me. How the hell do I convey "I came back for you" in knocks? How do I tell her I will get her out of there?

I place my palm against the smooth surface of the door. Sylvia and I barely talked this year. She was my partner in crime all through middle school and the first two years of high school, even while she fooled everyone into thinking she was an angel—even while she fell in love with a skinny white chick.

When Mamá got sick, Sylv became more serious. Then she spent most of last summer withdrawn and closed off from everyone. That's when I lost her. She stares at me sometimes, and I feel like we live in two different worlds. But on the rare days we find each other, I remember what it is to be a family.

She knocks again, slowly. I can feel the vibrations under my hand. It's another melody, that of a Spanish lullaby our mother used to sing to us when we were tiny. It's slow, sad, and hopeful, and fuck if it doesn't make me smile.

Another shot interrupts our song.

Silence.

No. No. *No*. If I could claw through the door, I would. I bite my lip to keep from screaming. We might as well be divided by a chasm—me crouching on the cold linoleum and her inside on the worn carpet.

I reach for the hammer. The alternative to picking the lock is forcing it. If I hit the shackle just right, it should spring open. The noise will alert people inside, but I don't know if that matters anymore. If I don't open one of these doors, they will die. We're already at the worst-case scenario.

I force my breathing to slow and relax my shoulders. I hold the hammer with both hands. It won't do me any good against guns, but it will do me a world of good against this cursed door.

I take aim at the padlock and pull back.

"Don't!" Fareed's loud whisper reaches me before I take a swing. He's flushed, his hair matted against his forehead. He clutches the bolt cutter as he bends forward to catch his breath. "Sirens in the distance. The police will be here soon."

I take a step back. With the tip of my sleeve, I wipe at the tears that have sprung to my eyes. Finally. We need the police here *now*.

"Are the doors open?" I ask.

Fareed shakes his head. "Two of them. Cutting all the chains would take too long, but we can direct people out. It's better than nothing."

I glance at the doors. Whether Far meant it or not, his words sting. He did what he had to do, and I failed—spectacularly. I take the bolt cutter from him. Now is not the time to beat myself up. "Let's get them out of here first."

Without another comment, Fareed reaches out and squeezes my shoulder. Then he takes a place at the side of the door and lifts the chain, his hands spaced so he can keep hold of the ends once I've cut it. I place the blades on half of a chain link, and with all the strength I have in me, I push down.

....

CLAIRE

Static crackles over the radio. Codes fly back and forth between dispatch and the various first responders. It'd be so much easier if I didn't have a clue what they were saying, but most comments are in plain English. Mentions of more cars, a road block. Opportunity only has two police cars, and backup from other towns isn't enough. Helicopters. Mention of SWAT teams and setting up an emergency response unit in the parking lot. Discussions of whether or not a bomb squad needs to be sent in.

And Matt is at the heart of it all.

None of it seems real. None of it sounds like something that would happen to us, to anyone we know. Not in Opportunity, Alabama. We have the occasional robbery, sure. We had a whole slew of car fires a couple years ago. But the voices on the radio sound as if they are preparing to lay siege to the school.

Our officer doesn't respond, apart from the occasional "Ten-four." Her eyes are focused on the car in front of her, and her hands squeeze the steering wheel.

Next to me, Chris stares at his hands. I'd talk to him, but I don't know what to say. I only have too many questions.

The side of the road blurs by my window. What seemed to be an endless stretch to us is only a matter of a minute or two by car—maybe even less than that. Soon we'll be back at Opportunity High, and for the first time since I started school there, the thought makes me physically ill. *What is waiting for us?*

I tear my eyes from the window and clear my throat. "Who called you? Was it someone on the track team?"

At least some of us succeeded, despite the odds. I always knew they could do it.

It takes a moment for our officer to realize I'm talking to her. She glances back at me. The flash of worry in her eyes makes me wonder how old she is, if she has friends or family at Opportunity. It won't be long until the whole town is anxiously waiting at the gates of the school. News spreads like wildfire in Opportunity. *Do Mom and Dad know yet?*

The officer shakes her head. "We got a call from inside the school. Several calls actually."

"Oh." My mind spins. *Did whomever contacted the police manage to get out? Were they safe when they called?*

"Do you know if anyone—" I can't bear myself to finish the sentence.

The officer clears her throat. "I'm not really supposed to talk to you about this. One of our deputies will debrief you as soon as we've set up the perimeter." I can hear what she doesn't say: *Because we don't want to start a mass panic or release unconfirmed information*. But I need to know what to expect.

Chris places his hand over mine. "We don't expect you to tell us the details, Officer," he says in his best polite voice. Everyone always sees Chris as trustworthy—he gets treated like an adult, while most of us high schoolers are treated as children. "We just want to know where our friends are and if they're safe."

....

SYLV

Tapping has never sounded more beautiful, but with hope comes more fear. Tomás might be able to help us, but only at the risk of his own life. We're trapped here, but the thought that he might be in danger because of me—always, always because of me—chokes me. He'd be better off running and never turning back.

With every step Autumn takes closer to Tyler, I wish Tomás would step back. I can't lose them both. Although he's a few minutes younger than me, Tomás has always been my defender. He was the brother who took me under his wing when Seve enlisted and Félix went to work in Birmingham, the brother who first got me into trouble and the one who'd get me out again. Until last summer, I never felt scared when Tomás was near.

On the other side of these doors, he is safe.

There is more to life than these walls, and Tyler can't destroy it all. I have to believe that. I can protect Tomás by pushing him away.

Because I can no longer protect Autumn.

My fingers trace the pattern on the wooden panel while my eyes follow Autumn. She moves fluidly, though every step brings her closer to certain death.

When Tyler fires another shot into the auditorium, she flinches but doesn't stop. This is what our world is now: the dead, the lost, the wounded. Could I have done anything about it? Could I have prevented this by speaking up?

At junior prom, Tyler walked up to me on the dance floor. Even though Autumn and I barely saw him anymore and he ignored me completely at school, he wanted to dance with me.

He demanded *a dance with me.*

It was not the first time he tried to flirt with me, but I could not dance with Autumn, and I did not want to dance with him. He intimidated me, and the very idea of being close to him left me on edge. I turned him down and fled outside to get some air.

He followed me out.

"Don't pretend you're not interested. I've seen the way you look at me, the way you move. You want me. Don't deny it." When he placed his hand on my arm, I whirled around to ram my elbow into him.

He caught me and pinned me against a wall. "Keep the hell away from my sister."

"Fuck off, Ty." I kicked against his shin. "I despise you. Get away from me."

He didn't. But that time, I did.

In Abuela's stories of brujería, witches and spells, Tyler would be possessed. Grief would've let the darkness in, and that darkness would consume him. It has, and now it's destroying us all.

Now he'll use Autumn to get to me.

Tyler's plan is revenge, which he'll get—not by killing us but by killing everyone we hold dear.

....

AUTUMN

Ty discards his cap and smooths his carefully styled hair. He still stares at the cowering boy, a soft smile playing on his lips. "Matt, won't you come out to play?" he asks. "I have a score to settle with your sister. And with my own sister, who wasn't even supposed to be here today. If only she'd just listened to me."

"Ty," I call out again, to be sure he heard me. My mind is screaming *Danger*, screaming at me to run and hide and pray he'll never find me. But I stand tall.

Ty gives me the look my father crafted for troublesome customers—equal parts business and pure disgust. "Do you expect me to shout at you from across the room? Did your mother not raise you better than that?"

I ball my hands into fists but wrestle down the rush of anger. I take a slow step. One more.

Someone brushes my hand in a gesture of support.

Another step. Another. Ty turns from Matt and levels the barrel at me. He smirks.

The closer I come, the more Ty—*my* Ty—drifts away from me.

In our stuck-in-the-sixties kitchen, complete with vomit-green walls, Ty grimaced at one of Dad's lame jokes. He rarely laughs anymore, but when he does, his eyes light up.

"I think I needed time to evaluate," Ty said with that smooth and careful voice of his. "I realize now that what I expected from OHS was unrealistic. I believe I can put things right." He methodically cut up the meat on his plate, positioning the bite-sized pieces in neat rows.

"I'm glad to hear that, Son," Dad said. He never called me Daughter, *but he always called Ty* Son. *"Your grandfather always said this town can be a hard place to live, but you've got to fight for it. A boy runs away when things get difficult. It takes a man to confront a problem head-on."*

Because that's exactly what Dad had been doing. He faced his grief. It's not like he hid behind alcohol and anger, scaring half the customers from the Browne store with his foul moods. Scarring me. Not at all. Not my dad. I would've rolled my eyes if not for fear of Dad catching me.

"Yes, sir," Ty replied.

I kept my eyes fixed on my plate and never said a word.

In retrospect, neither Dad nor I knew what Ty meant. I thought he planned to put things right with Tomás and with Claire. I was glad. He finally seemed like more of his old self. I was wrong.

A shot over my head jars me from my thoughts.

I'm staring at a stranger. This is not the same person who showed me the abandoned shed near the cotton fields, where I could dance in secret. This isn't the same person who bought me pointe shoes after my old ones were too worn to be used. He may look like Tyler and sound like Tyler, but this is not the same person.

It can't be.

"Move or I will shoot the boy."

He's a stranger.

With my full attention on the aisle, I take two, three steps. At the front of the auditorium, I bite my lip as I step over the body of a girl not much older than me. When I reach the stage, the full horror hits me, and I nearly double over. The bodies of half a dozen teachers lie up there, and three more who are injured are cared for by their coworkers. A junior slumps against the wall, his face gaunt, blood pooling from a wound to his shoulder. Nyah's lifeless body lies only feet away.

I freeze. I can't go any closer, no matter how much it's the right thing to do. I swallow. "*Why*, Tyler?"

With his pale eyes trained on me, he steps closer, and everyone who gets as close to him as I am will be able to see the same thing. His gaze is devoid of feeling, emotion—humanity.

He reaches out, grabs a fistful of my hair, and pulls me

onto the stage. "Why couldn't you just have listened to me?" he says so only I can hear.

I falter, but Tyler doesn't seem to care. "You think you are so special, don't you?" he snarls. "Do you even care about anyone anymore? Your family? Your oh-so-special girlfriend? Or do you only care about yourself?" He points the gun at my leg.

"Please don't." My cheeks burn so hot, they vaporize my tears. But I pull myself together and stare back at him.

"I love you," I whisper.

And then he smiles. His eyes twinkle, and he is the Ty I knew.

And it breaks me.

To: Sis

Come and get me. I want to go home. I want to go home. Pleasepleasepleaseplease.

CHAPTER TWELVE

CLAIRE

When the gate to Opportunity High comes into view, our car pulls to the side of the road. Other police cars pass us. Turning in the driver's seat, the officer stares both of us down.

"When we reach the school, there will be a safety perimeter. You are to stay outside of it at all times. Is that understood?" She waits for us to agree. "One of our deputies will come to talk to you. He'll want to know what you've seen, what you've heard, anything that might be of help. We'll have your full cooperation on this?"

Chris stares at me, and I cringe at the thought of talking about Tyler. The Tyler I knew. The Tyler I misjudged. I don't want to, but how can I stay silent?

"Yes, ma'am."

"We'll be setting up an emergency response center in town so you'll have somewhere to go." At this, her smile is a little wry, and for the first time, she sounds like a

worried older sister, not a police officer following proto-
col. "I understand you kids want to know what's going on.
I would too if it were my friends trapped in that auditorium. But for now, we can't share any information. I trust
you won't get in the way of us doing our job?"

Chris is the first to nod, and I force out a reply. "No,
ma'am. We won't." I hesitate and then add, "We can help.
We can draw maps. Show you—"

"No, it's too dangerous," she interrupts. "We have floor
plans. We'll do the best we can for your friends. We'll try
to keep everyone safe, but you can't be involved." The
frown on her freckled face fades, and her voice trails off.
With a curt nod, she turns back toward the windshield.
She glances over her shoulder and pulls onto the road,
leaving us in silence in the backseat.

Trapped in the auditorium. It makes sense. The shooting started about the time Principal Trenton's speech
would've ended, but somehow I never imagined that.
Panic and people running through the halls, yes. But the
entire school trapped and Tyler with a gun? Not in my
wildest fears had I considered that. And I wish I didn't
know now. The auditorium isn't a hunting ground; it's a
shooting range.

It's a morgue.

I curl my fingers around Chris's and lean into him. We
were even luckier to get out of assembly than I thought. If

it weren't for Matt, there'd be only one thing on my mind: go home, where it is safe. I'd hole myself up, call Trace, and wait for this nightmare to pass.

Instead, the car slows and turns into the parking lot.

In the front seat, the officer waves at another policeman taping off what must be their perimeter, and he motions her to carry on. Her hand sneaks out to the radio. "Ten–twenty-three. Arrived at the scene."

Just like that, we're back at school.

....

SYLV

Wild fury burns away my fear. If Tyler lays a finger on Autumn, if he harms her, I will curse him with Abuela's spirits and everything that's in me. I will kill him even though he would kill me first.

Torn between Tomás behind me and Autumn in front of me, the air itself compresses, and I can't breathe, I can't breathe, I can't breathe.

On the other side of the auditorium, two teachers slowly get to their feet. A handful of students a few steps below them rise too. In the middle of the group is the girl who helped lock us in.

The set of her mouth is fierce.

I thought the walls kept courage out, but maybe

they are actually holding it in. We're not just fighting for survival—we're fighting for hope and a thousand tomorrows.

At the edge of the stage, Autumn stands before her brother.

Her eyes flick from the gun to Tyler and back. Whispers swirl around me. "Did he say 'girlfriend'?" "But she…" "Do you think he meant…"

I hug my knees to my chest with one arm and reach for my bag with the other, as if it can shield me.

All Autumn cared about was dancing. All she cared about was me. But she never told anyone about either. Too afraid Opportunity might disapprove. Too afraid knowing her family would.

Not that their disapproval would've changed anything. Their relationships were already broken.

But Autumn never lets on how she feels. No fear. No anger. No happiness unless she's dancing. She's too well trained, too careful to slip up and give people the chance to hurt her, but I see her pain. I always have. I just wish she could see me like she once did.

For Autumn's fifteenth birthday, Mrs. Browne took Autumn and me to Birmingham to see a matinee. Autumn's mother was a few months away from returning to the UK as the special adviser on a new production of the Royal Ballet—though she never got there.

But Autumn and I were still blissfully ignorant of all that was coming. She was so excited to see The Nutcracker *that she talked about it for days. I was far more excited about seeing Birmingham and going to dinner at a fancy restaurant. While money had been tight for my family, it wasn't for Autumn's. Not back then.*

When the music started and the curtain came up, Autumn's face lit up. She could have been a star, she was glowing so brightly.

I think that was the moment I fell for her.

Onstage, the clock struck midnight and the Nutcracker came to life, bravely advancing his gingerbread men and his tin soldiers against the army of the Mouse King.

Rescued from death by a slipper, the Nutcracker fought, Autumn smiled, and my heart soared. I didn't know if she felt the same way, but after intermission, when the lights dimmed, my hand crept toward hers. She looked at me, then squeezed my fingers. In the near darkness, we held hands for the rest of the performance.

I was so happy.

That was the first and last day we were careless with our feelings.

Six weeks later, Mrs. Browne lost control of the car on her way to pick Autumn up from ballet class. Cause of death: exhaustion. Even at home, she worked long hours, and she barely slept. That night, frost had turned the roads slick, and the police said she must've dozed off before a patch of ice sent the car into a tailspin. She never woke up.

At least I could be who I wanted to be at home. When Mamá started to lose everything that made her who she was, she told us she wanted to remember us happy.

She wouldn't want us to give up without a fight.

I hope she'll remember us as being loved.

I slowly rise to my feet. I can accept what Tyler did to me, but I won't stand by while he hurts Autumn. She's been hurt too often. She needs to know she is loved.

....

TOMÁS

The chain doesn't snap into two. The bolt cutter barely moves under my grip. I should have gone to all my PE classes. The little strength I have is from a summer job placing fence poles. I always thought adrenaline would allow me to move cars and break wood planks with my bare hands. Maybe I'm not stressed enough. Maybe I'm stressed out of my mind.

The handles of the bolt cutters slowly pull closer together. Gradually, gradually.

Snap.

I wince.

Half a link done.

Fareed smiles his encouragement. He turns the chain, and I place the bolt cutter. This time it's easier. I know what to expect and give myself a better grip.

Snap.

With the chain cut, I place the bolt cutter on the ground and take one end of the chain from Fareed. We don't need words for what we're doing. As quietly but as quickly as we dare, we remove the chain from around the door handles—it loops through once, twice. The metal rings against the door, and every time it does, we hold our breaths. As long as we keep the chain steady, the sound shouldn't carry.

I hope.

When we remove the last loop, Fareed steps over to the other side of the hall, where he curls the chain on the floor.

I stare at the door. It'd be so easy to throw it open, but one set of doors isn't enough. I pick up the bolt cutter and wait for Fareed to take his place at the next door. Lather, rinse, repeat. Opening two sets of doors will be better. More students will be able to get out. Besides, the police will be here soon. We only have to hold out for a little longer.

I'm breathing heavily when the blades snap through the next link. No wonder Fareed looked so flustered before. My hands are shaking under the pressure.

"C'mon," Fareed says softly. "Only one more cut."

I nod.

"If you want me to take over…" He gestures at the cutter, but I place the blades around the chain. He's right—only one more. Besides, these doors are mine. If I do anything right today, it must be this. To give Sylv and everyone else that one chance in hell.

Snap.

....

AUTUMN

"I love you," I say, louder this time. "You're my brother. You're my best friend."

My words push against the wall Ty has erected around himself. His gun is still pointed at my leg, and he might as well threaten my life. "You're everything to me."

His eyes flick toward my face. As long as he's focused on me, the auditorium is safe. As long as he's focused on me, I might be able to get through to him. If I have to lie to him to reach him, I will.

"I swear I never wanted us to change. What happened to us, Ty?"

His eyes darken. "I lost everything."

"You never lost me," I whisper. I need a hint, a glimpse to prove that despite his actions, he is still my brother.

"You were the only family I had when everything changed. I knew it was hard on both of us, but you made me believe fulfilling Mom's dream—*my* dream—was still possible."

If I'd known he felt as lost as I did, would I have done anything differently? It was Sylv who gave me strength, dancing that gave me purpose. But, "God, Ty, I missed you so much."

If only he'd have let me in. If only he'd confided in me.

Ty blinks. "Believe in your dream?"

"To get out of here." A split second after the words leave my mouth, I realize my mistake. Ty begins to laugh, louder and louder.

"I wanted to be your excuse to stay home. I never wanted to hurt you." He shakes his head. "But you really don't care, do you? After Mom died, I had no one anymore. Do you know what it feels like to be all alone?"

I move out of the line of the gun, but I don't break eye contact. "Of course I care. Of course I know. I lost as much as you did. But it didn't have to be like that. You had Dad and me. You had Claire. You had friends."

"Lies! They all left me. I wanted to be part of your life, and you pushed me away too. It's too late for regret now."

I clench my fists and swallow, anger and fear rushing over me. "How could I possibly push you away when you were nowhere to be found? *You told me you'd protect me*."

"You told me there was nothing keeping you here. Not even me."

Get lost, Ty.

"So you decided Dad needed to teach me a lesson?" I mimic his voice, as I remember his grin and his careful calculation.

"It was a mistake. I told you I was sorry. Why don't you ever listen?" He squeezes the trigger. A bullet drills itself into the stage next to me, and I swallow a scream. The spell between us is broken.

"It was your fault," he says. "All of this, it's your fault."

The Adventures of Mei

Current location: On my way back

>> Opportunity is a good school. I liked it there. I was happy. Whatever you might hear today, the school, our town isn't the problem. Don't you dare put the blame on us. You have no right to judge us.

Comments: <37>

Mei, how do you feel about the accusations that the school could've done something to prevent this? Did you ever feel unsafe there?

OMG CAN'T YOU READ?!

I always loved your dad's classes. I hope all is well with him—and with you.

Can you call our hotline to leave your name and phone number? It'd help us to know who is and who isn't inside right now. You can also report yourself to one of our officers at the scene. They will be able to help you.

CHAPTER THIRTEEN

TOMÁS

Timing is everything. If we open the doors too wide, it'll be conspicuous. If we're too slow, everyone won't get out.

Fareed takes up position at the second set of doors, and I crouch where Sylvia and I tapped out our code. I inch open the door. Sounds of whispers, sobbing, muffled cursing filter out.

On the other side of the door, I see her. Her long black hair obscures her face, and she trembles as she moves slowly along the wall, her arms wrapped to her chest. But she's *alive*. Relief stumbles through me. It's all that counts.

Her eyes are fixed on whatever's happening onstage, and as I crawl through the doorway, I follow her gaze.

The first thing I see are the bodies. Principal Trenton. Mr. Herrera, our Spanish teacher. Other teachers. Other students. After finding Neil, after hearing all those shots, all this death shouldn't have surprised me. But it does.

And at the heart of it, Tyler. Tyler, who I thought was harmless. He clutches his gun, with a grin that chills me to the bone. *He's dangerous*, Sylv told me. What she didn't say was clear too—she was terrified of him. Was this why? Did she guess what he was capable of?

My fingers curl into fists, and everything inside me screams to attack him.

But his eyes are trained on his sister. As long as Autumn distracts him, she's keeping the rest of the auditorium safe. And with the doors open, we have more important concerns. We can get people out.

I place my hand on my sister's shoulder. Sylv turns. Her startled recognition and look of relief are the most beautiful things in the world. I wrap my arms around her and pull her close. She returns the hug, which makes me feel as if maybe I'm not such a screwup after all.

I point toward the door. She nods and taps the shoulder of the guy next to her.

One door down, Fareed alerts the girl closest to him. We crawl into the auditorium as shoulder taps ripple through the room. To the credit of shock or fear or common sense, no one stands up and rushes the doors. Instead, students back away with care. Those who are sitting as if they are still at an assembly make sure their seats don't creak when they fold up. They inch toward the aisles and the doors, poised for flight.

Sylv works her way toward the next block of seats, spreading the word one quiet sign at a time. And although I wish she'd run, to get out of here and be safe, I'm glad to know she's with me as we face what comes next.

....

AUTUMN

"Oh, Ty…" My brother—the lost boy.

In the auditorium, people are moving from their seats and toward the doors. I don't dare look too closely for fear of alerting Ty. But as long as he's staring at me, as long as he's ranting at me, the people behind him have a chance to escape. And as long as I'm staring at him, I can pretend the rest of the auditorium isn't here. I can open up.

The night of Mom's death flashes before my eyes. She was home between trips to Europe, and she was staying away longer every time. She was so tired. I didn't want her to drive me—I told her I could skip my lesson, but she insisted. I had to practice. She did not believe in wasting time. Perhaps that was why she was always traveling.

Perhaps she was only escaping too.

After class, I waited for her. The other parents came and picked up their kids. I called home, and Ty told me

Mom was on her way. But no one showed up. Not until the police found me dozing in the locker room.

By then, Mom was already gone.

And I was the only one left to blame.

"I know it's my fault," I whisper. "Not a day goes by when I don't miss Mom. I wish I could go back and redo that day. But I can't. I *can't*. I can only keep doing what she wanted me to do, and she wanted me to dance, Ty. You know how much she cared about that."

"And so you kept on dancing."

"It's the way I remember her. It makes me feel close to her." I grasp at the first memory that comes to mind. "Remember we went to see *Othello* last year? Remember how you drove us to the river after the show, and we sat there watching the sun set? The sky was perfectly clear, and everything was peaceful. It was the first time in a year I didn't have to worry about Dad. It was the first time in a year I felt safe.

"You gave me that. You saved me." *Let me save you*.

The hand with the gun trembles. He lowers it ever so slowly.

For a moment, I break eye contact to glance at his gun. I can't help but wonder if I could lunge and take it from him, if *that's* the way to stop him.

Ty tucks a strand of hair behind his ear and shakes his head. "No, Autumn."

He starts to turn, and time slams to a stop. In the aisles, students are crawling toward the doors, away from the cover of the seats. They're targets.

Before common sense—or survival instinct—kicks in, I reach out to grasp Tyler by the shoulders before he can see what's happening.

"Tyler, look at me. Listen to me."

The hand with the gun jerks. His finger squeezes around the trigger. The sound bounces off the walls, and I recoil. Ty's face hardens.

His arm snaps back, and the barrel of the gun bashes my cheek.

Spots of light burst in my vision. Pain blossoms over my face. Blood pools in my mouth.

I hold my hands to my cheek and whimper. The metal taste makes me gag. I spit.

Ty bends over me so our faces are inches apart, and I can't stop myself from shaking. Ty's breath warms my face and chills my bones. "You're too late to save me now."

....

SYLV

A gash opens across Autumn's cheek, and blood trickles out. Tyler raises his hand and strikes her a second time.

She squares her shoulders and looks up at him defiantly. *Don't fight it. Don't fight him.*

We'll fight him instead. Tomás, Far, and me. We'll stop him. We'll save everyone.

We'll create our own happily ever after.

I reach out for Tomás's hand—but he's three rows down already. Around me, students are moving. I crawl toward a group of freshmen huddling together. I tap their shoulders, place my finger to my lips, and point at the doors.

We're not out of the school yet—not by a long shot. But when we are out of the auditorium, we'll be closer. There'll be exits everywhere around us.

Across the room, Fareed catches my eye. *Of course* he's here with Tomás. He nods in quiet support, and for a moment, I dare to believe everything might be—not okay. It'll never be okay again—but possible.

We're escaping.

Adrenaline rushes through me.

The girl next to me looks to be the youngest of the group. Her eyes well up, but her face splits into a grin so wide it makes my heart ache. She leaves her bag and follows her friends between the seats. They slide past me toward the door.

Holding hands, they slip out into the hall. They got out. *Madre de Dios,* it's real.

....

CLAIRE

From the outside, Opportunity High looks like an old-fashioned building, with its redbrick walls and large windows. Most of the classrooms are on the sprawling ground floor, with the library, science rooms, and study halls up on a smaller second floor. The gym and sports grounds are visible from this side of the parking lot. The auditorium is on the other side of the building, by the faculty parking lot.

We pass Jonah's car and Tyler's, and grief stabs me.

Matt's figurine still stands proudly on Jonah's dashboard.

An officer stands, coordinating the emergency vehicles just beyond the cars. All around us, people are working quickly. The police have taken charge. Officers are setting up a roadblock. A SWAT team is circling the school. A large tent is being erected in front of the school, with vans and cars parked all over the grass.

This looks more like a military operation than any drill JROTC has ever run. It's overwhelming. It's a siege.

Our police car is ushered toward an area cordoned off by cones and caution tape. We park near one of the vans, and an older guy with a deputy's badge waves us over.

Our officer—I still don't know her name—gives us a literal push in the right direction and mutters something under her breath, though I can't make out what. *Good luck* maybe. Or *I'm sorry*. Either seems appropriate.

I'm not sure I want to know what's waiting for us here.

"C'mon," Chris says softly. "We can do this. Look there."

I push my head up. Behind the deputy are three familiar faces.

At least Coach and the others are still safe.

Jay Eyck
@JEyck32

I skipped school today. I'm not at #OHS.
Pls stop asking me questions. I don't know
what's going on.

10:19 AM

Jay Eyck
@JEyck32

I can't believe it. Never thought this would
happen at our school.

10:19 AM

Anonymous
@BoredOpportunist

@JEyck32 You're so naive. Don't believe
everything people tell you. There's always
more to the story.

10:19 AM

Jay (@JEyck32) ➜ Kevin (@KeviiinDR)

Dammit, Kev. Tell me ur okay.

10:20 AM

CHAPTER FOURTEEN

TOMÁS

I crawl low, staying close to the ground, whispering so as not to attract attention from the stage. "The doors are open. Keep quiet. Alert others. Get out."

Other times, I simply tap and point. The auditorium is so large and there are so many students, I doubt we'll reach everyone. But every life we save counts.

Teachers who had sat with their classes signal students to get out as well, and for once I'm glad they're here.

The floor is hard beneath my knees as I creep forward, and the rough fabric scratches at my hands. Fareed has moved much farther down already.

On the stage, Tyler leans over Autumn. It's not just the gun that makes him imposing. He's dressed as if he is going to a formal event. Even from the back, I can tell that his dress shirt is nicer than anything he could have bought in Opportunity. His pants are pressed. A magazine with bullets is tucked into his waistband. He always dressed with care, but today he's particularly polished. Did he drive to Tuscaloosa to pick out this outfit? Is it easier to kill people when you look good? I eye my torn jeans and T-shirt.

I can't wrap my mind around Tyler. I don't want to. But I wish I'd done more than ram his head into a locker after last year's junior prom. I'd do anything to end this.

He was never one of us.

In front of Tyler, Autumn pushes herself into his face. She doesn't give any indication she saw me or the open doors, but I think she has. I hope she has.

Autumn's so quiet and so measured, I don't always understand what my sister sees in her. But it doesn't stop me from feeling protective of her. She makes Sylvia happy, and that's all that matters.

After Sylvia withdrew from me over the summer, Autumn and I talked. When my sister started to avoid me, I wanted to make sure someone looked out for her. Autumn promised she would—and she does.

Now she's looking out for everyone. As long as Tyler is occupied, we can get students to safety.

I tap the guy next to me, Rafe, our linebacker. He flinches and curls his body to protect the girl beside him. His face is streaked with tears. When he sees it is me, he raises his eyebrows.

"Get out. Run," I whisper.

Soon, *soon* we will be out of here. Tyler will forever

haunt us, but he won't be able to harm us anymore. We will remember that we escaped. A weight lifts off my shoulders as people scramble out. It gives me wings. I wish I could run through the aisles. It would make for faster work, but people in the seats are starting to notice the movement. Word that the doors are open spreads steadily through the auditorium.

I reach out for the next person. We're so far from the doors now, we're crawling targets. If I ever had any purpose in high school, this is it.

This is how I shape our future.

....

AUTUMN

"I hate you," Ty seethes. "I wanted you to stay, but you never cared about me. You never cared about any of us. You only ever cared about dance."

I wince. I want to contradict him, but I can't. Dance is beauty. Dance is compassion, honesty. The only way I've ever known how to share my feelings is through dance.

But he digs the barrel of the gun into my ribs. "So dance. You wanted a stage. Take it."

The last thing I want to do in the face of Ty's hatred is dance, but with his eyes on me, the people in the auditorium can get away.

161

So I take up fifth position. I haven't warmed up, and the tension in my shoulders and legs makes it almost impossible to move. Behind Ty, the faces of my impromptu audience are far clearer than they should be—full of anger and judgment. I'm beyond being afraid that people won't understand me. This is the one thing I can do to help them.

I freeze. I don't know which solo to choose. Not one of the classical solos Mom danced. Not anything I prepared for Juilliard. If I make it out of here, I don't want him to have tainted those steps.

But I have nothing else.

I slide from fifth into fourth position. I brace for him to shoot me, but he doesn't. Ty is still watching, so I let the rhythm carry me as I fall into *tombé,* one step, two step. My knees tremble, but the moves are familiar. My Chucks squeak on the stage's wooden flooring.

I close my eyes and pour my memories of Ty into my dance—his worried frown when I told him I still wanted to dance. His strong arms around me when I woke up from another bad dream. His promise when he gave me my ballet charm: *I believe in you.*

When Mom's sister came to visit for the holidays, she brought our cousin. Three-year-old Alex held on to Ty's hair when he carried her around on his shoulders and clung to his hand whenever he set her down. Peals of laughter lit up our house for the first time since Mom died. Dad stopped drinking for a whole day.

I cling to those images, but they all turn dark. All that's left is Ty's smile. His smile when Dad threatened to break my legs once and for all so I'd stop dancing, while Ty leaned against the doorpost without a protest. The smile when he shot Nyah.

I fold into myself. I'm forever trying to get away but incapable of cutting myself loose.

And then I see her face. Sylv's the only person who matters. Our late summer nights are the only time I've been happy.

My steps become brisk and bright. My movements become more brazen—until, in my mind, she turns away too, and our dance follows the familiar rhythm of the lies we've told each other.

My ankle twists, and the movements become harder.

Mrs. Morales is getting sicker each day. Soon she won't be able to care for herself anymore, won't be able to recognize her children. Tomás told me Sylv is considering staying in Opportunity because their grandfather can't care for Mrs. Morales alone—and I never told her I supported her. Whatever she decided to do.

I never told her the idea of coming back after I'd escaped chokes me, the idea of losing her breaks my heart.

Instead, we stuck to false truths. *"How are you?"* *"Good, I guess. Don't worry."*

I slow. I swallow a sob. I'm not sure if I pushed her away or never had her at all. I just know I've never been so alone.

I look out to find Sylv in the auditorium. Then my feet are swept from under me, and I land flat on my back, staring up at the barrel of Ty's gun.

....

SYLV

I tap the shoulder of the sophomore in front of me who'd been arguing with his mom on the phone when Tyler started shooting. He sits with his head in his hands, oblivious to what's happening around him.

"The doors are open," I whisper.

He raises his head and stares straight through me. His eyes are bright green, bordered by his black eyeliner. I can't even remember if I've seen him move since Tyler started shooting. His phone still lies on the ground where he dropped it.

I snap my fingers in front of him. "Pay attention."

His gaze focuses on me. I point first to him, then toward the door, then toward the people down the row from him. "Take as many people as you can with you, but get out."

When he doesn't seem to comprehend me, I sit back on my heels and recall what he said earlier. "Do you want to find CJ?"

"Find CJ?" he repeats slowly. His voice is hoarse.

"What's your name?" I ask.

"Steve."

"Sylvia. The doors are open. She'll be out there," I promise.

He straightens, but he doesn't move, as if he's forgotten how.

"Can you do me a favor?" I nearly drag him out to the aisle. I point to Asha. She sits, leaning against the wall, her arms wrapped tight around her waist. No matter how many people pass her, she does not move. "That girl over there lost her sister today. She needs to get out of here. Can you make sure she does?"

It's a trick I learned from dealing with Mamá's illness. Whenever she zones out, the best thing to do is give her specific tasks, small tasks—feed the dogs, collect eggs, keep an eye on the oven while the cookies we made together bake. It's not infallible, but when she feels disoriented and overwhelmed, those tasks keep her from panicking. I hope it'll help now. Because someone needs to get Asha out. It's the least I can do for her. We're all responsible for each other.

"Please, please get her out," I say.

Steve nods.

And for the first time, I believe I can *do* something. I can change this. I've been so afraid I was losing everything, I nearly lost myself. But I'm remembering now. I'm remembering, and I'll never forget.

The open doors give us hope, like a gulp of fresh water after a day's drought.

While Steve makes his way to Asha, I continue to spread the word. As long as Tyler's eyes aren't on me, I can move freely—and he'll regret it.

....

CLAIRE

Uncharacteristically, Coach wraps an arm around us both. He's a few shades paler than he was when we left him, but he plasters on a smile. "You make me proud, kids." He always tells us that after every race. Whether we win or lose. He tells us we've made him proud, and he goes on to tell us how we can do better.

Today, he just squeezes our shoulders. Behind him, Esther sits with Avery, who has her leg held high and a bandage around her ankle. They smile wanly.

"Any word yet?"

"You two were brought in by Sergeant Donovan, yes?" the deputy cuts in before Coach can answer my question. It takes me a second to realize Sergeant Donovan must be our police officer. I squint at his name tag—W. H. Lee.

Chris nods. "Yes, sir." He keeps his voice neutral. "She didn't tell us much about the situation inside though."

"Good." The deputy walks to a van that appears to be a hastily assembled command center with computer equipment and radio control. He picks up a clipboard. "If you'll follow me. We've already debriefed your coach and the others, but we have a few questions to ask the two of you."

He leads us away from the rest of the team, and together we head to the far side of the parking lot. It's quieter here, although this little patch of grass gives us an excellent vantage point to see the cars speeding toward Opportunity. None of them are police cars or SWAT vans. They're sedans, pickups, sports cars, even a tractor plows down the road. The roadblock stops the vehicles, but it doesn't stop the parents.

Opportunity gossip is just as effective as any alarm system. Not that it surprises me. Plenty of kids must have called their parents instead of the police, and in Opportunity, gossip spreads without care for family or creed. Even the staunchest enemies come together to share the latest news. On either side of the tape, the parents form an honor guard of despair.

"We can help," I say before Deputy Lee can ask us

anything. I hop from foot to foot from nerves as much as trying to keep myself warm.

Deputy Lee doesn't respond to my offer. He glances at the clipboard instead. "We'd like to know what you saw and heard before you left the premises. How many of you were there?"

He must have heard this story from Coach, but it appears he's under orders to double-check the facts. Or triple-check. It makes me wonder if they think we could be part of this, but I can't even wrap my head around that. Not when Matt's inside. Not when we just ran halfway to Opportunity.

"There are five of us, sir," Chris says with a quick glance at me. "Coach, Esther, Avery, Claire, and me. The varsity runners. We have a track meet coming up in two weeks, and Coach wanted us prepared."

"Did you see anyone? Hear anything?"

"Apart from the shots, no. The track is on the other side of the school. It's secluded," he says. "We didn't see anyone enter or leave the building."

"Is it common for you to miss the principal's start-of-semester speech?"

Chris smiles. "Once track season starts, we eat, sleep, and breathe track. And considering our winning streak, Principal Trenton is always happy to give us extra training time."

Deputy Lee glances up. "Have you been in contact with anyone inside?"

We both shake our heads, but his question makes me realize that we could. My phone's still inside, but there will be other cell phones here I could borrow. I could call Matt. I can. I will. I have to know he's safe.

Deputy Lee leafs through his notes and then he frowns. "Does the name Tyler Browne ring a bell?"

My stomach drops.

Jay Eyck
@JEyck32

"What did you do when you heard the gunshots?" I didn't. IM NOT @ #OHS.

10:29 AM

Jay Eyck
@JEyck32

"Do you know what drove the shooter?" I. DON'T. KNOW. #leavemealone #please

10:29 AM

Jay Eyck
@JEyck32

IF YOUVE NOTHING HELPFUL TO SAY GTFO OF MY FEED.

10:30 AM

234 favorites 127 retweets

CHAPTER FIFTEEN

TOMÁS

Two rows down, I see a familiar face. Jennifer, gorgeous captain of the cheer squad, sits in a seat at the end of the row. Jennifer, whom I've had a crush on since the day I met her. She's tall and athletic with ebony skin and eyes the color of the night. These past four years, she's noticed me exactly never, though I've tried to catch her attention.

Believe me, I tried.

Now she's here. And safe. Euphoria tugs at my lips. Maybe it's adrenaline, maybe it's plain stupidity, but life makes the most sense to me if I do not have to take it seriously. And I want to make the most of every moment.

Fuck. If I'm going to be the hero today, I'll make sure she notices it, inappropriate timing or not.

I slide on hands and knees up to her chair and tap her hand, gripping the armrest. Her lips are set in anger, not fear, and it only makes her more stunning. She nearly jumps, although she's sensible enough to swallow any sound.

I put on my most charming smile. "Hey, want to go out? The doors are open." She stares at me like I spoke Spanish instead of English, even though I'm pretty sure I didn't.

"Doors," I whisper, falling back to my script and pointing. "Get out. Take your friends."

This time, Jennifer nods and elbows the girl next to her—another cheerleader. The news gets passed down the rest of the row, and the girls sneak up the aisle. Jennifer is the first to pass me, without even acknowledging my existence.

In the next row, students and teachers alike are alerted by the movement, and they turn too, restlessly and too loud. Their seats spring back to folding. Gesturing wildly for them to keep silent, I barely have time to feel disappointed by Jennifer. But it doesn't mean I'm not.

I didn't expect her to fall for me like a knight in shining armor, but I would have liked a smile or some indication that I'm helping to save her.

I head to the next row.

A manicured hand squeezes my shoulder, and I whirl around, almost colliding with Jennifer. She doesn't smile. She's still tight-lipped and pale. But she mouths, "Thank you."

Then she turns and heads up the aisle and out the door

with her friends. I don't move from my crouch. My heart hammers, and it isn't from fear or dread.

It's because she'll know who I am when I ask her out next time.

....

SYLV

At the back of the auditorium, Fareed stands near the door, ushering people out to keep the lines moving. He's a clear target, and it doesn't seem to bother him.

On the far side of the auditorium, those who are unharmed help the wounded walk—at least the ones who can still move. Some of Tyler's bullets were harmless, ending up in the walls or in the ceiling. But the first few rows and the aisle by the door where he came in are filled with the injured and the dead.

I can't even remember how many times Tyler unloaded his weapon. Rationally, I know there have been moments when he didn't shoot, when he spoke poisonous words instead. But the echo of gunfire still rings in my ears.

Part of me wonders when Tyler will be stopped—and what will be left of us when he is. Part of me wants to follow the others out of the auditorium, to be far away and safe.

But if I turn away now, with Autumn getting to her feet

in front of her brother, I'll always be looking back. And I refuse to be afraid anymore.

So I touch shoulders and whisper while my eyes are focused on the stage.

I refuse to watch her die.

Next to me, a student stands and starts ushering people out as well, murmuring soft words. Another student follows him, and another. Between them, they help a girl who clutches her arm to her chest. They shield her as she moves toward the door.

This is who we are now—terrified and unafraid.

I keep moving down. My mind keeps cycling through memories, creating fragments of a story—my story.

Autumn's fingers entwining with mine.

Tyler's hands pushing me down.

The letter burning a hole in my pocket.

Tomás coming back for me after all those months I pushed him away.

No matter how this plays out, these moments are all part of me. It's time to stop hiding.

The only two people who matter now are in front of me—the boy who broke me and the girl who put me back together. I will not let him take her away from me again.

....

AUTUMN

They say your life flashes in front of your eyes right before you die. As I wait for Ty to pull the trigger, no memories overtake me. No last wishes or if-onlys. I cower. My shoulders hunch; my hands tremble. When Dad was at his worst, he'd call me every name he could think of and wouldn't stop until he felt like he'd won.

Ty is worse. His eyes are wild and unrecognizable.

He shakes his head. It's as if we're the only two people in the auditorium. "I thought you understood the loneliness and the loss. I thought that was why you wanted to get out—to fight back. To *win*. You know how much it hurt to find out about you and that—that slut? You've been lying to all of us."

I smile sadly. "You can blame me for Mom's death if you want. Believe me, there is nothing you can say that I haven't already thought myself. But it was an accident. A terrible, terrible accident." I raise my voice. "But me and Sylv? We're no accident."

Whatever happens, I want her to know that. I want her to know I loved her, I *love* her, and I wish I would have told her a thousand times over. I wish I'd told her how I felt before today came crashing down around us.

"She makes me feel safe—like you did once. She doesn't judge me. And if you can't understand that, I'm

175

sorry. I am. But it doesn't change how I feel about her. I love her."

If Ty wants truths, that is the simplest truth of all. And with every word I speak, with every secret I tell, I win and another student slips out of the auditorium.

The silence that meets my words pins me to the floor; it is ice and fire and hope. I brace myself and whisper, "I loved you too." Despite everything, I still do.

I expect him to snap after I finish my monologue. Instead he hesitates and blinks, as if awakening from a reverie. The barrel drops for a second. Maybe I got through to him after all. But Tyler's lips curl into a snarl.

"Too little," Ty says, "too late."

My eyes widen and my hands tremble. And this time, there is nothing I can do when he spins around, his gun poised, and faces the thinning crowd in the auditorium.

....

CLAIRE

"We can't get a clear picture of Tyler's motivation, so we are looking for anyone who might know him well. We've sent a team to his house, but we are looking for a student perspective too," Deputy Lee prods. He isn't local, otherwise he'd know all of this.

"His sister's a junior here," Chris says after a moment.

"Autumn's a quiet girl, but everyone in Opportunity knows her. Everyone knows the Browne family. Their dad owns a store on Main."

Deputy Lee looks from Chris to me and back. The deputy says, "Had Tyler not dropped out, he would have been a senior with you two." There's an unspoken question in his words, an understanding that we must know more about him.

I remain silent. It's as though admitting we dated will make me responsible for what has happened today. Ty, whose beautiful smile once lit up my every day. He used to be hopeful. But right now, I can't even remember him happy.

I guess I am responsible for this. In a way we all are. I have to speak up.

"Tyler used to be my boyfriend," I manage at last. "Though I don't know what I can tell you. We broke up at the end of school last year. We met here at school. We were working on a project together when he asked me out, and I liked being around him. He made me laugh. He made me feel like I mattered."

One afternoon, he waited for me until JROTC was done. He sat on the hood of his car with a paper bag next to him. It almost looked as if he were bringing me lunch. But when he saw me, he jumped off the car and spread out the bag's contents in the sun. Pewter figurines. Little

177

bottles of paint. Brushes. He practically bounced. "*I found these in town last week. I thought Matt might like to give it a try. You know, for his birthday.*"

I was so happy, I could've kissed him then. In fact, I did.

"But his mom's accident changed him. He was withdrawn. Grieving. He told me it felt like the world was crumbling around him. After his mom died, we only hung out at school or at my place. He seemed happier there. He loved being with Matt."

I loved him... I think.

Deputy Lee stares at his clipboard. His expression doesn't reveal his thoughts, but I feel my cheeks heat. Despite everything, I want to tell him this is not the Ty I knew.

Chris takes a subtle step closer until our shoulders touch.

"How long were you together?" the deputy asks.

"Two years."

"Was he ever angry or violent with you?" His questions almost seem to follow a checklist: Signs of Irrational Behavior 101. "Do you know what upset him today?"

I wish I did.

Some fifteen feet away, people around the command center start shouting. When Deputy Lee turns up his radio to ask what is happening, the unmistakable sound of gunshots is audible in the background.

I start forward involuntarily, but Chris moves in front of me. Deputy Lee turns the radio back down again.

Go in! I want to tell him. *Help my brother.* I swallow and try to answer his questions as best I can. "Ty didn't really fit in. Some of the other students used to drag him into fights. I think he was scared."

"Did he express a desire for revenge?"

I hang my head. "He told me he'd show the world. He told me we'd never forget him. But I only thought he meant he wouldn't let anyone get to him."

Deputy Lee scribbles something on his notepad. "Did he ever discuss any of his plans with you?"

"He used to skip assembly because he thought the auditorium was a prison. But how could I—"

"So you didn't know he was planning this?"

"Of course not!"

Chris squeezes my hand.

"Have you spoken to him recently? I understand he dropped out." His voice grows softer, and it only makes me feel worse because there's one thing I haven't told him, haven't told anybody.

"After we broke up, we didn't talk much. I saw him around town occasionally when I needed supplies at the Brownes' store, paints and tools for Matt—my brother. Ty was better with customers than his dad. Everybody knew old Mr. Browne started drinking again after the accident..." I swallow. "Ty had bruises. He wouldn't talk about it, but it wasn't because of the fights. They were welts, like someone hit him. I think his dad did."

A sudden burst of anger forces out the next words, and my voice trembles as much as my hands do. "Sir, I can tell you about the Ty I knew. But I had no idea he would do something like this—*could* do something like this. I don't know why it happened. I wish I could've stopped him. I would've done anything."

If Deputy Lee is disappointed, he hides it well. He nods. "Are you willing to speak to one of our detectives later for a more in-depth interview?"

"Yes, sir."

"We ask that you to stay in the area that's been cordoned off until we've found a suitable place to gather the survivors."

I wince at the word *survivors*. "My brother is inside. I need to do something to help."

"I'm sorry. We need you to stay off to the side while we deal with the situation and set up a triage system."

A new message emanates from Deputy Lee's radio. This time, he doesn't wait; he sprints back to the command center.

Out of habit, I look at Chris for direction and find him staring at me. He shakes his head.

We may have our orders, but we are not going to stand by and wait. I nod, and we run after the deputy.

To: Sis

It hurts.

To: Sis

You must not have your phone. You would've called me. But I want to talk to you. If you can, if you find some way... I hope you're safe.

CHAPTER SIXTEEN

TOMÁS

Tyler faces the auditorium. At his feet, Autumn crawls out of the way.

We all freeze, waiting to see who will make the first move.

Damn it. Damn him.

Tyler stares at the open doors, the students making their way up the aisles. Then he laughs. "No."

A bullet shatters one of the overhead lights, and glass rains down from the ceiling in a deafening roar.

"I. Will. Not. Let. You. Go." Tyler punctuates every word with a gunshot.

The students next to me scramble toward the door, ducking to keep low. The people nearest the doors run and push to get out. Mr. O'Brian, one of our science teachers, wraps his arm around a freshman as he escorts a group up the aisle. A bullet skims his shoulder, and Mr. O'Brian stumbles but manages to stay on his feet. Dozens of students spill into the hallway, yet too many are left behind.

Screams ricochet as bullets land around us.

Tyler fires at random, emptying his gun before he reaches to change the magazine. We wanted to free the auditorium and instead we brought more death and destruction. So much for heroism.

I scan the crowd to find my sister. She's in front of several other seniors, just below the chaos. She's standing right in Tyler's line of sight, but she doesn't duck. And somehow, miraculously, his spray of bullets misses her.

Rage consumes me.

He won't touch my sister. Never again.

Then Tyler glances over his shoulder at Autumn. She's crawling away, her back toward him. It'd be so easy to kill her.

Sylv darts forward to climb the stairs to the stage. Sylv, who refuses to be afraid of anything. She squares her shoulders and takes her first step toward Tyler.

A hand grabs my arm to stop me. "We need to take cover," Fareed says. "This is our chance. We need to get out."

Pure terror surges through me, stronger than anything I've felt today. "I can't leave Sylv! He'll kill her." I try to wrestle free from Fareed.

"You can't help her if you get shot," he hisses frantically. Far drags me toward the door as the firing starts again. "She's distracting him. She's giving all of us a chance. And you are not going to ruin it by dying now, dammit. Come *on*."

Sweat pours down Far's temples. "Autumn's still down there," he says, softer now. "She'll be in a better position to protect Sylv. The police will be here soon."

His fingers dig into my shoulder.

A freshman beside us stumbles and trips, sliding against the seat when a bullet perforates her neck. I almost join the screaming as blood spatters my face.

Fareed is right. And I hate him for it.

....

CLAIRE

Outside the cordoned police area, the road in front of Opportunity High has turned into a war zone. From inside the school, we can hear a mix of gunshots and screams. The air around the school stills, as everyone—police officers and parents—take in what it means. Officers pull assault rifles from their vans while three BearCats screech onto the asphalt, with ambulances hot on their heels.

Behind the barriers, news crews trickle in, setting up cameras and prepping anchors. "We are looking at a live picture of Opportunity High, home of a school shooting that has shocked the country. With the SWAT teams preparing to enter the school, parents have gathered to await news of their children and…"

The camera lights brighten the area around us, zooming in on everyone who so much as moves.

As we follow Deputy Lee at a distance, Chris and I inch past the camera crews, trying to ignore them. I wrap my arms around myself. "Is this what we are now? A story on the news?"

Chris hesitates, then stuffs his hands into his pockets. "They're vultures."

Beyond the camera crews, parents are pressed against the barricades. They call out to me or to anyone who will listen, despite the dozens of agents fielding their questions. "No, sir, we can't tell you anything about your son or daughter yet." "Yes, ma'am, as soon as we know anything, we will inform you." "Sign your name here, and we will cross-reference it with our list." "We do not need another contact inside. Please try to remain calm."

"*Claire!*" My heart leaps at Dad's voice. *Would he have come home early from work? Is Mom with him?* But when I scan the crowd, all the faces blur together, an Impressionist rendering of despair. Dad is nowhere to be seen. I want him to protect me, like when I was a little girl and he would hoist me on his shoulders when I got tired — but then he'd know I'm not as brave as Trace.

I do not want him or Mom to be here.

Chris and I move closer to where the police officers prep. Not so close to the command center that we will get noticed but not too far off either. We're both waiting to hear if there's something, anything we can do. If I can't be courageous, I need to make myself useful.

The sheriff in charge is directing the SWAT officers, and the wind blows fragments of conversation our way, wrapping itself around Chris and me in icy gusts. We don't reach out to keep each other warm.

Something changed between us, and it scares me. "Talk to me. Please."

For the past four years, Chris and I have been best friends. Only a couple months ago, he drove me halfway across the country to see Tracy before she left for the desert. He arranged places to stay, food to eat when I couldn't think of anything but my sister leaving for the other side of the world. He cares for Matt like his own brother, especially after Ty and I broke up. I need him close.

Chris's eyes darken, and he stares past me. "We all have a lot on our minds," he says softly.

A shout swells through the parents, press, police, and I turn, almost missing his next words: "I'm so terrified to lose you."

One set of double doors slam open, and students come running out.

....

AUTUMN

The thunderstorm of bullets shatters any inkling of hope. Anytime I feel as if there are no more superlatives, that we've reached the worst, Ty proves me wrong.

He fires round after round. Those who are close enough to the door run for their lives. Those close to the stage hide in the corners and sides of the auditorium.

On hands and knees, I crawl away from him as fast as I can. With every inch gained, I expect a bullet to shatter my spine. My knees and my elbows feel like Jell-O under my weight, but I pull myself forward, clambering toward the steps at the side of the stage. I don't want to look down at the carpet, which is stained with blood. But I need to get away from here. I need to get to Sylv before Ty sees her. Because if he does, there will be nothing left. If she dies, I will never be able to tell her that she is the one who keeps me standing. That her lips taste like a promise. That she makes me want to be a better version of myself. If she dies, I will believe every ugly word Dad ever said about me.

I slide between two rows of seats and fight the urge to cover my ears. A red-haired girl next to me shakes uncontrollably. Dried blood smudges her cheek. She reaches out and squeezes my hand. I choke back a sob.

Past the red-haired girl lies the boy Ty threatened earlier. Matt. For all the time my brother and his sister dated, we never officially met. Ty rarely brought people home, and he stopped altogether after Mom died. Whether it was because he was ashamed of me or of Dad, I never knew. Maybe he was ashamed of us both.

Matt's shoulders knock against the chair legs, he's shaking so hard. He looks so vulnerable, so scared. I reach out to him, then pull back. My brother is the reason he's terrified.

Matt looks up, but instead of the disgust, the anger I deserve, he smiles.

I crawl closer to him. He clutches a phone, and I wrap my fingers around his ice-cold hands. "I'll protect you."

It's a lie, but it's kinder than the truth. The blood on his T-shirt has soaked the fabric, which stands out bright against his chalky skin.

"Take me home?" he asks.

I nod and stroke his hair.

And.

Silence.

Letting go of his hand, I push myself up to peek over the seat. Ty casually discards another magazine and reaches into his waistband for another. In that heartbeat, when Ty's gun isn't loaded, I breathe. My mind calms.

But in the circle of destruction around him, only one person is close enough to stop him. Sylv.

No. No, please.

She walks up the aisle toward my brother. Sylv is out in the open. There is nothing between her and Ty as he snaps a new cartridge in place. Still that doesn't stop her.

Please don't.

Matt squeezes my hand. And we brace for whatever comes next.

....

SYLV

The echo of Autumn's words spurs me on. *I love her.*

For a heartbeat, I wish I could lunge at Tyler and stop him, but he'll shoot me before I can even move. His anger pushed me into darkness over the summer, which has been devouring me.

I stand tall.

"Grief is one big, gaping hole, isn't it?" I say quietly. I don't even know if he hears me, but my words are as much for myself as for him. "It's everywhere and all consuming. Some days you think you can't go on because the only thing waiting for you is more despair. Some days you don't want to go on because it's easier to give up than to get hurt again."

I'm losing my mother one day at a time. I'm losing Autumn, who isn't just my girlfriend but also my best friend. "I've lost myself. You took everything from me. I've stared at the abyss, Ty. I know everything about grief. And I'm so, so sorry for your loss."

Tyler stares at me.

At his gun.

"If you want revenge, take it out on me." I swallow. "But you are not alone."

Behind me, I hear someone make a dash toward the door. Tyler pulls the trigger and shoots, and the thud of someone falling is followed by a loud silence. "Yes, I am."

The next shot passes so close to me, the hair on the back of my neck stands on end. I swallow a scream. Another bullet tears at the carpet near my feet. And I breathe in the too-familiar scent of expensive cologne and putrid sweat.

All the fear I've been keeping at bay rushes over me. The next bullet will be mine. I know it will be, but I won't stand to face it. I want to savor every breath. I turn and run.

Someone cries out. Someone shoves into me; someone else holds out a hand to steady me.

Tyler's footsteps follow me. I'm almost at the door. Everyone else is hiding, crying, and holding on to each other. With every step, I push forward harder.

Step after step.

Only one more.

Familiar hands grab my arm.

Tomás pulls me out of the auditorium, kicking the door

shut behind us and bracing against it while Far closes the other set of doors.

The next bullet drills itself into the heavy wood with a dull thud.

I launch myself at Tomás. I want to pound his chest and tell him he was a fool for risking himself. He shouldn't have done it for me. Never for me. But my arms wrap around his shoulders. He smells of horses and home. He startles—then he returns the hug. My brother. No matter how far I push him away, he will pick me up again and piece me together.

"Te extrañé." I whisper the words into his chest.

"I missed you too," he replies. His voice brims with feelings.

Those four words shatter me, but on the other side of the door, someone curses. More gunshots. We can't stay here. We can't keep the doors closed with too many people still inside.

My hand slides into Tomás's, and this time I am running, dragging him and Fareed with me. The hallway offers nowhere to hide, so I instinctively make for the staircase. The air around us zings with life and possibilities—and I want to keep it that way.

We run away from the screams.

We run to get far, far away, where we'll be together and safe.

CJ Johnson
@CadetCJJ

If I had a gun, I'd kill him. I would. #OHS

10:34 AM

Abby Smith
@YetAnotherASmith

@CadetCJJ We're all here, praying for you.

10:34 AM

213 favorites

George Johnson
@G_Johnson1

@CadetCJJ THEY'RE COMING FOR YOU.
THE POLICE ARE THERE TO HELP.

10:35 AM

Anonymous
@BoredOpportunist

@CadetCJJ If you shoot him, you're just as
bad.

10:34 AM

34 favorites

CHAPTER SEVENTEEN

CLAIRE

"Stand down!"

Everyone in the parking lot makes a beeline toward the students pouring out of the school.

"Stand down!" The SWAT commanders and the sheriff shout over their radios, close to where Chris and I are standing. They must have snipers in position.

Hovering in the safety between the cars, I count the students as they make their way out. They come in groups of ten or twelve, a few lonely duos. They emerge supporting each other, some of them covered with blood. They raise their hands high as soon as they see the police.

Two seniors stumble out: Rafe, our star linebacker, and a girl I vaguely recognize as a Mathlete. They make an odd couple. Rafe's head and shoulders taller, but he's leaning on her. They're followed by a trio of girls from Matt's year. I've only ever seen them together, and I've only ever seen them smiling. Right before the holidays, they asked Matt if he wanted to watch a movie sometime. I think one of them has a crush on him. They didn't stop giggling, and Matt didn't stop blushing. But today they're grim and pale—and Matt is nowhere to be seen.

If I could, I'd run and demand to know if they've seen him.

If I could, I'd run into the school and drag him out myself.

One of the SWAT officers makes his way toward the school entrance, gesturing. "Get those students out of the way and get a situation report ASAP."

Several police officers guide the students toward the medic tents on the side, away from prying eyes. Ambulances are lined up and waiting to carry the wounded to the hospital.

I watch the doors. After the initial rush, the occasional student walks out—face blank and confused. Blood stains most students' clothes. One guy hesitantly backs away when he sees the officers coming toward him. Another girl breaks down in tears as soon as she crosses the threshold.

The trickle of students brings us to a hundred, maybe, but no Matt.

Chris brushes my arm.

I pull back. "I can't—I can't deal with waiting. There must be *something* we can do—help take down names, care for the—our *friends*. I can't just stand around!"

I look over to the gathering crowd, and I tense. Mr. Browne stands alone. The other parents leave space around him, as if his pain and fury could burn those around him. Everyone knows by now. Everyone must know.

His son is endangering their children, and he is guilty too.

When our eyes meet, I move before Chris can stop me.

The police officers reach Mr. Browne before I do and pull him to the perimeter, which is the only thing that saves me from making a scene.

Catching up, Chris wraps his arms around me, equal parts restraining and reassuring me. But I keep repeating the same thing over and over into his chest. "You ruined him. You ruined him. You ruined him."

Chris simply holds me tighter until I don't have any strength left, and I start to cry. He pushes a strand of hair out of my face. "You should've told someone about the welts, Claire. He needed help; they both did. But you can't tell yourself that is why Tyler did this. Most abuse survivors don't commit massacres."

"Do you think it would've made any difference if I'd stayed with Ty?"

Chris winces. "No. I don't think there's anything any of us could have done."

....

SYLV

We crouch halfway up the stairs, out of Tyler's direct line of sight, but close enough to keep an eye on him. We need to follow the main hallway out of the school, but Tyler's left the auditorium, announcing himself with more gunfire, and he's prowling, waiting for those who escaped to come out into the open. Like the unlucky student who tried the exit by the sports fields and must've found it locked. When he came running back, a loud shot sent him sprawling across the floor.

"We have to go upstairs," Fareed whispers.

"But we'll be trapped there," I counter. "There's no way out."

From the sounds below, Tyler turns toward the main entrance—and I pray that anyone who may have dawdled got out. At least he moves away from us. But we're still trapped.

I understand what he's doing now. Autumn and Tyler lost their parents. And because of me, they also lost each other. As long as he thinks I'm in the building, he will come after me. The knowledge no longer fills me with dread.

"We can go out over the roof," Fareed suggests, nodding at the stairwell. Tomás opens his mouth to interrupt him, but he hurriedly continues. "If we try to make it to the front of the school, Tyler'll find us, and he won't hesitate to shoot us."

A moment of understanding passes between my brother and him.

"We need to get out of the school as fast as we can," Tomás says finally. He glances my way, and I feel his eyes burn. "The police are outside. If we get to the roof, they will help us."

I stare at a kid lying in front of the doors to the auditorium. The bullet tore straight through his *Dark Side of the Moon* shirt. He blinks. His breath comes in loud, rasping gasps, racking his whole body. Time is no longer his. He's merely holding on because he's too afraid to let go.

What will he dream of?

My hand creeps toward the Brown acceptance letter. Out of habit. Out of comfort—while the boy's breathing quiets and he slips away.

I hope he's found peace.

....

TOMÁS

I pull Sylvia toward the stairs. Fareed trails us. We sneak rather than run.

It's foolishness to go to the second floor, but it's the best option we have. Fareed is right—the hallways are too exposed. There's simply no place to hide. The roof is safer. Besides, if Tyler ventures out there, the police will be able to stop him.

Shots ring out. They sound close—too close. But then the sounds grow fainter again. We let out a collective sigh.

Sylvia's unstable on her feet. She clings tightly to my hand.

"You came for me," she says. "You came back for me. I can't believe you didn't just run."

Her words hit me hard, but I don't think she notices. We've grown so used to pushing each other away, even these circumstances can't prevent us from doing so. But then, there's comfort in the familiarity. I fold my hand over hers. "I will always come back for you."

She shivers. "When Autumn—I never thought—" she stammers. "Yo no sé lo que nos pasó."

"This has nothing to do with you," I say. Even though we both know it's a lie. It has everything to do with her. With Autumn. With me. It has everything to do with all of us.

She's refused to speak about whatever happened between her and Tyler at junior prom last year. They argued on the dance floor, and he followed her outside. She never told me what he said or what he did, but I know he hurt my sister. She came back trembling and afraid. I'd never seen her afraid before. And that Monday at school, and not for the first time, I slammed him against the lockers. He spit and told me to get my hands off of him. I told him I would put him in a full-body cast if he ever touched my sister again.

He didn't respond, and the students around us never even glanced our way. When the first period bell rang, I let him slide to the floor. He wasn't in my English class later that day. He didn't show for any of his classes, and I didn't see him again—until today.

I thought it'd been a relief to both of us. I never realized she was still scared—not until this morning, which feels like an eternity ago. "*He* had nothing to do with you. You never saw him again after junior prom, did you?"

Sylvia looks away, and she closes herself off from me, just like she did last summer. And it's as if all the pieces of a puzzle slip into place.

She came home late that night. I sat on the porch with Mamá and told Sylv I made tea—for once in my life—and she threw up. She stayed in bed for days, and when she emerged to face the world again, she wouldn't face me. And I never knew why. I could only guess. Of course I could guess.

I just didn't want to know.

"Tomás." Fareed snaps his fingers in front of me. "We have to keep moving."

Sylvia nods, and we push away from the walls around us, from the smell of gunpowder. It isn't until we reach the second floor that I realize Sylvia never answered my question.

....

AUTUMN

The second Ty left the auditorium, two students began arguing about whether or not to barricade the doors. The bickering gives me a headache.

"What if he comes back?"

"But then we couldn't get out."

"We need to keep him out. That's all that matters!"

Still, no one tells them to stop. I raise myself up to survey what's happening. The remaining teachers are all occupied with the wounded. The dead are scattered across the auditorium, but survivors appear, rising from the corners, crawling out from between the seats. Some care for the injured, applying pressure to stop the bleeding, using their shirts as makeshift bandages. Others seem frozen in terror. Their pale, tearstained faces all focus on one point.

Me.

They look at me in helplessness, anger, loathing, and fear. Wherever I turn, there are people staring. Not just students but teachers too, as shell-shocked as the rest of us. There is no one here I can call a friend.

I stare at Matt, who lies shivering between two rows of seats. If I stay here, who will stop Ty from hurting Sylv? Who still stop Ty from hurting himself?

My brother and my girlfriend. I feel as if I am losing them both. It tears my heart in two.

But Matt's counting on me. If I follow Ty, who will take care of him? I crouch between the seats. "Can you get out?"

"I'm stuck, I think," Matt says. Although he is trembling, I can't tell how hurt he is, but he's visibly relaxed with Ty gone. "I can't move my legs."

I pick up his crutches and move them out of the way. "Reach out to me?"

He places his phone on the floor and wraps his hands around mine. His grip is surprisingly strong, and it's not hard to pull him into a half-sitting position. "Thank you. I don't know if I could have done that by myself."

I don't have the heart to tell him he couldn't. I wince at the red that's seeping through his shirt. I can't leave him. "Wait here."

I stuff my trembling hands in my pockets and turn on my heel, walking carefully past the stage. The lectern stands forlorn, Principal Trenton's glass of water forgotten on one of the shelves. On the far wall hangs a first aid kit. I've used it a few times for cuts and bruises before dance practice, when I couldn't tend to my wounds at home.

The kit is large and heavy, and it's been here since this school was built. I open it and spread the contents across the floor, trying to think of the most sensible way to handle this.

In the auditorium, the volume rises. Other students are speaking up. "The police are here." "Help is on the way."

"If you can run, run," I suggest, raising my voice. "If you stay, we need to keep everyone safe. Treat the worst wounds first. Whoever's not injured, help make the others comfortable. Does anyone here have first aid training?"

"Who put you in charge?" a sharp voice asks from across the room. CJ, who helped lock us in. I thought she was a hero for the way she handled that. She stares at me with hatred. "He's your brother. How can we know you're not like him? You didn't do anything to stop him."

"She tried," another voice cuts in, though I can't see whom it belongs to.

I bow my head and grab some bandages to help Matt. CJ is right. I am responsible. She can hate me all she wants once we've survived this. "Who's talking to the police?" I ask.

Several people raise their hands or their phones. "Can you tell them the situation? We need some EMTs in here with stretchers."

Even if it's the only thing we can do.

To: Trace

I'm not sure when you'll read this. I just wanted to say that seeing you on my birthday was the best present ever.

CHAPTER EIGHTEEN

TOMÁS

"Here's how we'll do it," Fareed says, alternating glances between the staircase and the hallway in front of us. The doors at either end of the corridor are closed, and the lights are dimmer here. "These classrooms have emergency exits to the roof. We need to find an open room and barricade ourselves in. You two start here. I'll take the other end of the hallway. Keep quiet and wave when you find something."

Sylvia looks like she's going to protest when Fareed smiles and says, "Don't worry about me." He taps the wall with one of the screwdrivers he's carrying, and his accent comes through more than before. "Have you seen me? Who would want to hurt me with these gorgeous eyes? You make sure you're safe." He stares at me as much as at Sylvia.

"What if none of the doors open?" she objects. The second floor has only one long hallway, which circles around the auditorium. The science rooms on one side have window access to the roof over the first floor classrooms. The study halls on the other side have roof access to the front of the school. But regardless of which roof we'll choose, it'll be harder to protect ourselves if Tyler shows up again.

"Well, the alternative is dying, and I'm not in the mood for that today." I rattle at the door, and when it doesn't open, I lean back and kick it. My heel doesn't budge the lock.

Fareed says, "We've come this far. We won't back down."

"Oh, Obi-Wan Kenobi, what would I do without you?" I roll my eyes, but I actually feel better.

"Admit it. I'm your only hope," Fareed replies. And it's true. He's been my partner in crime since the very first day. He stood by me when Tyler and I got into fights but also when Mamá began to slip away. He kept an eye on Sylv when she didn't want me close.

We check the doors down both sides of the hallway. After the gunshots in the auditorium, the rattling of locked doors somehow feels just as loud. But we make quick work of the doors. And when Sylvia catches my eye, I risk an encouraging smile. Between the three of us, there's no one I'd rather be with today. Together, we'll get out. Together, we'll survive this. Together, we'll be strong enough to face whatever comes our way.

This is where it ends.

....

AUTUMN

It's impossible not to listen to the hushed phone conversations. It's impossible not to wonder what's being said on the other end of the line. "We can't help you"? "Help is on the way"?

I walk back to Matt and pass the row where Nyah's body lies. I can't look at her, not when grief and guilt overwhelm me at every step.

I crouch. "Matt? How are you holding up?"

He shivers. "Okay."

"The SWAT teams are here," a boy on the phone exclaims. "So are the police. They'll be inside soon!" His words raise a soft cheer. And then he starts crying big, choking sobs that turn into laughter and back into tears.

"See, we'll get out of here." I wink at Matt, and immediately it makes me feel stupid—like he's eight instead of a underclassman.

His smile is a little fainter now, but it's real. He straightens his shirt, and when his hand comes back bloody, he stares at it. "Oh."

I want to say something, anything, but what is there to say? "I'm sorry my brother shot you"? "I'm sorry I couldn't do anything about it"? Instead, I just nod at the phone next to him. "Maybe you should try to call home."

Right when I say that, the phone lights up with an unknown number. Matt stares at it, but he makes no attempt to pick it up. "Can I?" he asks, terror stealing his voice.

I can't help myself—I smile. "I think it'll be okay."

When the display goes dark again, Matt touches the phone as it if may burn him. "Will you go after Ty?"

I sit down next to him and wrap my hand around his. I shake my head. "I will but not yet. I'll stay here with you. Until they get you out."

"Thank you."

The phone vibrates again.

"You're safe, Matt."

He picks up.

....

CLAIRE

"Matt?" My voice breaks. "Are you all right?"

I sit down on the concrete and clutch the phone Chris produced for me—from one of the officers or one of the parents, I don't know. I hear Matt's heavy breathing, and when he speaks, his voice sounds distant, duller. "Claire? I hid under the seats. He never saw me."

"I was so worried—I'm so sorry I'm not there—I'm so glad you're okay!" I trip over all I want to say to him.

I want to reach through the phone to make sure he's really safe. "Matt, I'm here with the police. Everything will be okay, all right?"

I'm pretty sure Matt nods, like he always does when he's on the phone. Then he clears his voice. "Tyler's gone."

"Tyler's gone?" I repeat. Chris leans over to listen too. *Ty shot himself?* My heart lurches.

"He ran out of the auditorium." I close my eyes, grateful that Tyler is okay, despite all that's happened, but Matt's voice grows softer with every word. I should comfort him, but this information is important. It could help the SWAT teams.

"Where did he go?"

"I don't know. I'm not sure if he plans to come back. He won't come back, will he?"

"Of course not." I gesture for Chris to get one of the police officers when another voice cuts in.

"He won't come back. He must know the police are outside. He'll be looking to get out."

My breath catches. *Autumn. Ty's sister.* I don't know her well, but Ty often talked about her. She was always the most important person to him. "Autumn?"

"Hi, Claire," she says dully. "I'm sorry."

I bite my lip. "Me too." With my free hand, I scribble what Matt said onto a piece of paper and then add *Autumn Browne*. Chris runs over to the command tent, where everyone stares at the school's blueprint. An officer nods at Chris, and they walk toward me.

"Will they get us out?" Matt asks.

"Of course," I respond. "The police are coming to help you. You'll be safe, Matt."

The officer throws a pointed glance my way, trying to get my attention, though I'm not ready to share the phone. "Matt, hold on a sec."

"Is that your brother?"

My hands tremble. "Yes, sir."

"Can I speak to him?"

I hand over the phone, and the officer starts talking. I pull my hair out of its ponytail and shake it over my ears to give my hands something to do—something that doesn't include grabbing the phone back and running off with it, because that's all I want to do. I need to hear Matt's voice. I need to know he's safe. I need to tell him everything will be all right.

....

SYLV

When the initial rush of escaping the auditorium passes, the silence of the hallways overwhelms me. I can't believe Autumn's still there. I can't believe we left her behind.

A year ago, a few days before Thanksgiving, Tomás,

209

Abuelo, and I threw Autumn a surprise birthday party. Mr. Browne had taken Tyler out of town for some trade show, and I knew it was the best present they could have given her, but I wanted to give her my own gift.

By midnight, we'd eaten all of Abuelo's cooking and finished the last movie in our cheesy dance flicks marathon. It seemed as though all of Opportunity slept as I walked her home. From my house to hers was perhaps ten minutes, nothing more. Apart from the occasional porch light, the houses were clad in darkness, which gave us the illusion of solitude.

I wanted nothing more than to kiss her, but instead, we held hands. It was the bravest thing we'd ever done.

"It's the witching hour," Autumn said. Her smile slipped away, and her eyes grew distant. "Do you suppose there are ghosts in Opportunity? Secrets that linger? Legends that will remain after we're all gone?"

Her words sent a chill down my spine, but before I could answer, she changed the topic. "I'm auditioning for Juilliard. I don't know how yet, and I'm probably insane for thinking I have a chance, but I need to try. Will you help me?"

I stroked the palm of her hand with my thumb. I hated that she felt as if she had to ask me. "Of course I will."

"Good." She smiled, though the shadows obscured most of her face. "Because if I stay here, I don't think I'll

matter. When I die, I want to leave a legacy—the Royal Opera House, the Royal Ballet, a small company in an open-air theater somewhere, even a drama school in a small town. But not Opportunity. Not in some place where I don't belong."

"And you won't have to. We'll get you in," I said, though selfishly, I wanted to keep her in Opportunity. Because she made me feel human and loved and important. But Abuelo always said there were two types of people in this world: those who belong to the soil and the good, rich earth, planting their seeds to blossom, and those who belong to the road and the endless horizons, carrying their home on their shoulders wherever they go.

Life turned Autumn into one of the wandering, and she was becoming restless.

But when we reached the dark porch of her empty house, she was still beside me and she was still mine. And before she could think of a hundred and one good reasons why we should be careful of what the neighbors might see, I leaned in, cupped her cheek in my hand, and kissed her.

Jay (@JEyck32) ➔ Kevin (@KeviiinDR)

Kev, please

10:38 AM

Jay (@JEyck32) ➔ Kevin (@KeviiinDR)

I wanted to ask you to prom, you know.
You wouldve laughed at me. (But hopefully
you wouldve said yes.)

10:39 AM

CHAPTER NINETEEN

AUTUMN

The phone lies in front of us on speaker.

Matt rests against my knees, one hand clamped around mine. This leaning position seems to be the most comfortable for him. He's seen the blood spread across his shirt, but I don't think he understands how serious it is. He treats it as a mild annoyance.

The auditorium is quiet. Even during the brunt of Ty's anger, students were whispering and whimpering. This silence is comfortable for the first time.

The police will be here soon, and I'm lulled into thinking normal life will resume again. Tomorrow will be a day like any other, as if this nightmare never happened.

When the officer on the other end of the line tells us to hold, I lean my head against the seat—the cut on my cheek throbs, the pain spreading across my face—and squeeze Matt's hand. "Feeling better?"

"I knew Claire was waiting for me," he says. "She had

track practice. She was grumbling about it all morning. She hates the cold." He is silent for a moment. "I told Chris to slip some ice down the back of her shirt if he could."

His matter-of-fact tone makes me smile, but I can't deny his voice is fading. And I don't know what to do except keep talking to him. "If I had a brother like you, I would be waiting with snowballs at the ready. Though you'd probably be far better at throwing them than I am."

He shifts against my legs, and I feel him relax. "Do you think it'll actually snow? I'd like to see it at least once. Tracy—my older sister, who's in the army—told me it snowed when she was in elementary school. Days in advance, everyone stocked up on groceries as if it were the end of the world. School got canceled and the shops closed. And then it snowed. Big, fluffy flakes. For about two hours." His laugh turns into a cough. "So everyone had the day off for nothing."

I remember that day. Mom taught me how to make snow angels, though there was barely enough snow. I was mesmerized by it all, but I hated how the cold seeped through my coat and clothes. It was the last time we had real snow, not the frosted dew we mistake for snow these days.

Matt continues, "Claire wouldn't have a snowball fight. When Tracy left, she forgot how to have fun. She worries too much."

"Maybe we all do," I say. *Maybe we all worry about*

our siblings too much. "When Dad shouted at me, Ty would listen to me. When I missed Mom, he would comfort me. He always told me he'd take care of me. I wish I could have done the same for him."

I don't know why I tell him this, but it feels good to say it out loud. Matt's quiet for a long time. When he speaks again, his voice has faded almost completely. "You shouldn't blame yourself for what your brother chose to do. That's what Claire told me when Tracy enlisted. I was so scared. I didn't want her to go, so I pushed her away. But Claire told me Trace didn't do it because of me. It was her choice. And I could support her, but I shouldn't feel guilty."

I squeeze his hand. "You're a fantastic brother. You make them both proud."

He tries to turn to me, but he's weak. My fingers remain wrapped around his; it's the only thing I can do to keep him from slipping away from me.

"Autumn?"

"Yes?"

"I'm so tired."

....

TOMÁS

Inane school policy. Why lock all the classroom doors between periods? No one in their right mind would try to steal OHS property. The textbooks and clunky school computers are not worth the trouble.

We make it to the corner before gunshots echo from downstairs. We freeze, Fareed jiggling a door handle, Sylvia standing in the middle of the hallway. The shots come closer, and I drag her into a doorway with me because she can't become his next victim. She struggles as if she doesn't realize it's me, then stills.

Fareed edges toward our side of the hallway. "We have to keep moving," he whispers.

"Ms. Miller's classroom?" I ask.

He nods.

I grab Sylv's hand and pull her with me. We rush toward one of the last doors, with its trademark singed lock. I accidentally "broke" it before winter break. Or more to the point, I blew it up.

Now I push open the door with ease. Although we won't have to worry about being locked out, we can't lock ourselves in here either. But Far's right. We have to keep moving.

I drag in Sylv, and Fareed shuts the door behind us. He leans against it, and we all pause for a moment. I hear no footsteps, but I doubt we would hear someone approaching who didn't want to be noticed. That scares the living daylights out of me. Tyler could be here any moment and we wouldn't know.

I take in the room.

The heavy lab tables are in fixed positions, making it impossible for us to use them as barricades. Sylv pushes against one of the tall cabinets, but it doesn't budge. She trembles and seems to deflate.

"Could we have stopped Tyler?" she whispers.

I sigh. "With superpowers maybe?"

Sylv rolls her eyes, and in any other situation, she would've replied with a string of Abuela's favorite curses. "That's not what I mean." Her exasperation makes me want to hug her.

At the same time, I can't help but ask myself similar questions. *Did we do the right thing? Did opening the auditorium doors give people a chance or did it cause more deaths?*

"We all did the best we could," I tell her.

"But what if—"

"This isn't your fault. No one can or will blame you. Unless you stay here and we get shot, because, in that case, I won't let you hear the end of it. *Come on*, let's get the windows open," I whisper-shout.

I move across the room and flip the locks of a window. The roof outside is flat, but there is no space to hide. Tyler only needs to stand at the windows to shoot us.

Fareed climbs on the windowsill and beckons for Sylvia.

She hesitates. "What if I could have had him arrested?" Her voice is almost inaudible, but it stops me in my tracks.

She won't meet my eyes.

I grow cold all over. "Sylv, what did he do to you?"

....

CLAIRE

The doctors, the police officers, the news crews, the parents—a hush falls over the crowd. In front of the school, three SWAT teams prepare to enter the building: one to safeguard the area and two to make their way to the auditorium. The police have already warned us that they won't be able to carry out the wounded until the school is secured. It would make the injured targets. But they will take care of them, and they will save as many as they can.

I stare at the phone that still lies in front of the police officer and me.

Oh please, let Matt manage to walk—run—with crutches. Even if he is tired.

I need him home so I can be the sister he thinks I am.

Chris places a hand on my shoulder.

On Matt's birthday, Chris and Matt played on the lawn. Matt had lent a set of crutches to Chris, so both held their balance on one crutch, using the other in a mock battle.

Their breaths formed clouds in the cold, but neither wore their coats, to Mom's dismay. Matt didn't care about the cold. He jumped, though his legs could barely carry him. He ran without fear of falling. And Chris treated him like the little brother he never had, chasing him and being chased. It was so nice to see them both so happy.

I got Matt's Star Wars*–themed birthday cake out of the bakery box.*

"They'll spoil their appetite if we get that out now," Mom said, putting plates on the table.

"For fries? I don't think that counts, Mom. Besides, the way Matt's been running around, he'll eat a horse." I stuck my head outside and shouted, "Dinner!" across the yard, then started to put silverware at each place.

"I'd be relieved if he did. He's been feeling nauseous lately."

I glanced at her. "Are you sure? He hasn't lost weight."

She gave a curt nod. "Dad and I have to talk to his pediatrician. If it has to do with his kidneys, he might have to be—" She swallowed the "hospitalized" as Chris and Matt came blundering into the kitchen. Mom gave me her best we'll-talk-about-this-later look. With Dad working long hours to pay for the medical bills and Tracy overseas, Mom confided in me more and more. And I hated knowing that even the smallest, stupidest infection could threaten my brother's life, simply because the lupus caused his immune system to have trouble multitasking—situation normal, all fucked up.

I'd have preferred to stay blissfully ignorant than face the possibility of losing Matt.

"Awesome..." Matt stared at his cake. "We need a picture!"

Mom took her camera off the counter and zoomed in on him and Chris standing on either side of the cake. Mom makes scrapbooks, and recently, Matt had taken over that hobby. At first, I thought it weird, but when Tracy left for training, I began to understand the value of tangible memories.

As we sat around the table, Matt at Dad's place since he was working late again, a slice of cake and honorary Han Solo figurine on a plate in front of the computer for Trace, the sun set and dusk fell. Within our circle of light, we were a family. I wanted it to be like that forever. Not Matt writhing in pain and Mom comforting him until he fell asleep and she went back to her room to cry until Dad came home. But like Trace taught me: If you're afraid, think about tomorrow, because tomorrow will be a new day. Tomorrow, there'll be new chances. Tomorrow, I'll be home.

Screams ring out over the phone, then Autumn's voice. "They're here, Matt. The SWAT teams are here."

I sob in relief and lean against Chris. I'm ready for a new day, a new start. I look up and touch my lips to Chris's.

He stills. Then he follows my lead and kisses me back. It's as if I don't know where he ends and I start.

This is the first thing that has felt right all day.

"Don't ever leave me," I whisper.

"Not in a thousand years." His words are warm on my skin. He leans in and kisses me again as if the world were ending. And actually, it has.

....

SYLV

"Sylvia, what did he do to you?" Tomás repeats.

He stands in front of me, his eyes flashing. They're so like Mamá's, brown with flecks of green. He slams his fist into the wall, and it breaks through all the words we haven't spoken these last few months.

Before Mamá fell ill, life was brighter and Tomás and I were inseparable. One summer, when we were twelve, we stayed at the farm and sneaked out almost nightly to search for lost treasures on the farm and in the woods. Mamá didn't know, and Abuelo slept through our ransacking—or pretended to at least. We had the best adventures together—until I climbed the roof of the garage on a dare, fell off, and sprained my wrist.

We were so scared. I didn't want to wake up Abuelo or tell Mamá, but the pain made me sick. We hid. Tomás climbed through the kitchen window to get ice for my arm and to raid the cabinets for snacks while I waited in our old tree house.

When he came back, we drank lemonade and ate candy bars until we couldn't stand them anymore. Tomás folded the wrappers into airplanes. The pain eased.

As dawn chased away the darkness, we sorted all the night's treasures—some marbles, an old pair of shoes, and the almost-whole skull of a fox. Tomás only cared about the skull.

"It's a part of history," he said.

"It's a fox," I countered. I held up the shoes, ancient leather hiking boots. "But this? This is a story."

He rolled his eyes, and I grinned. "Not just a story but a secret. And all these secrets are ours to keep."

He's always protected me. If we die here today, I don't want him feeling like he failed me.

I reach out to him and curse myself when I feel tears trickling down my cheeks. I don't want him to know Tyler raped me for the same reason I don't want Mamá to know. I want her to remember me happy. There was nothing either of them could have done to stop him. Opportunity has so many secrets.

The only thing that matters now is that we are together—we are alive.

"Nothing. He did nothing."

The Adventures of Mei

Current location: Opportunity High

>> I've never seen so many families and friends of students in one place. Not graduation. Or prom. There are even some of my former classmates. Graduates who never left Opportunity. We hold on to each other.

Students run out of the school. There are survivors—thank God there are survivors. But that makes it harder somehow. There are so many faces we don't see. Are they lost to us? I don't see my dad. I can't see him anywhere. We all cling to our lifelines. Our phones. Our memories. Each other. I feel so useless here. None of us have any answers.

Comments: <disabled>

CHAPTER TWENTY

AUTUMN

When the door to the auditorium bursts open, students scream. I lean over to see what's going on. Half a dozen officers dressed in SWAT uniforms sweep down the aisle.

I gently prop Matt up against a backpack. His face is ashen, the angles drawn sharper than when I first saw him. His lips are turning blue, distorting the words he wants to say.

Another half-dozen SWAT officers follow behind the first group, fanning out across the auditorium. They signal to indicate the space is secure. One of the officers closest to Matt and me curses under his breath before reporting the situation on his radio.

I rock to my feet and shout for someone to help me. I bend over Matt to hear what he's saying, but the words die on his lips, and his eyes begin to lose focus. I smile in the hopes he can see me, in the hopes he'll think I understood him. "When it snows, we'll have a snowball fight and drag your sisters into it," I say. "They won't refuse—not when I tell them how brave you were today."

Something sparks in his gaze—a smile that never reaches his lips. His eyes turn away from me as one of the SWAT teams approaches. I step aside, and he crouches by Matt, examining him.

"Can you help him?"

Under the visor of his helmet, the officer wears a tight-lipped frown. His eyes are concerned. "We'll need to get you and everyone who can run out of here as soon as possible."

I shake my head. "But can you help *him*?"

"When it's safe, we'll send in the paramedics for the wounded."

I stare at him, and almost imperceptibly, he shakes his head. "Let's get you out. There's nothing we can do."

"You can't be serious." I back away from him.

"Come on. You have to get out," he repeats.

Matt is pale, but he nods slowly.

All over the auditorium, students and teachers are guided toward the exits. Those who can still walk, walk. Others lend support. And those with serious injuries are left behind in a room full of death.

They won't let me stay with Matt, but I can't just leave either. Not when Sylv may be wandering the school somewhere. Not when Ty is still around. Because

225

Matt was right: Ty is my brother. He'll always be, no matter what.

The officer guides me to a group of students at one of the doors who are waiting for the go-ahead to be escorted through the school. No one makes eye contact, and it's almost a relief. If they're all so focused on getting out, no one will try to stop me if I try to stay in.

....

CLAIRE

Chris's lips move, but I don't hear what he says. I cling to the phone. Over the voices from the auditorium, I only ever hear the question: *Can you help him?*

Nothing we can do.

Chris places his hand on my arm, but I shrug him off. "Matt?"

It's silent for such a long time that I'm convinced it's too late. Then there's a soft cough. "I'm so cold, Claire."

I find an empty folding chair and sit. "I didn't know you were hurt."

"I didn't want to tell you. You worry too much."

I try to smile. "Punk, that's what I'm here for. I'll always worry about you."

"He didn't shoot me on purpose," he says. "He—" Matt starts to cough again, but it sounds faint.

Tyler *shot* him. My ex-boyfriend shot my brother. And Matt still tries to protect him—like *I* tried to protect him.

"Save your strength," I tell him quietly. "They'll come back for you. And I'll be here. I'll be waiting. You know how I promised you we'd decorate your figurines? We'll do that when you're home. The doctors will fix you up. They always do." My voice cracks, but I try to mask it. "When Trace is home on leave, we'll take a trip to the beach together, the three of us. Just like we used to."

Matt coughs again, but I imagine he smiles. My head feels so light, like I'm still running and haven't been able to breathe for days.

"I'd like that," he says.

I wish I could hold him close and tell him everything will be all right, because between Tracy and me, we'll always take care of him. But how can I tell him that now?

"You know, out of the three of us, you were always the cool one. You're creative. You're so brave." I'd always meant to tell him that. "I'm so sorry. I should be there for you."

Chris crouches next to me. He always knows exactly when I need him most.

My words are met with silence. I wait to give Matt time to catch his breath, but I can't hear him breathing anymore. "Matt?"

My fingers are ice-cold.

"Matt?"

"Matt!"

....

SYLV

A gust of cold air blows in. "We'll be fine on the roof," Fareed decides as he leans out. "There's not much cover, but if we're close to the building, from inside it shouldn't be too obvious that we're out here."

I swallow a sudden bout of nausea. We're trapped in this lab. I'd rather be trapped in the open air—even if it is up on a roof. Even if we could lock the window—which we can't—all Tyler would need is one bullet or the butt of his gun to shatter the glass to get to us. Still, it's the only option we have other than running back into the hallway, and that would be death for us too.

Fareed is climbing over the sill. "At least it's not raining."

With Fareed on the roof and Tomás inside, they help me maneuver through the open window. It's a little too high to climb out easily, and I'm not as nimble as Autumn would be, but I get a leg up and over.

Once I'm sitting on the windowsill, Fareed walks away, looking around him. Presumably to find police officers. To signal for help. Tomás wraps his arms around me. "We're on top of a roof. Are you afraid?"

"Not of heights right now." I try to smile, but I don't quite know how. "The roof itself doesn't scare me, but there's nowhere to hide up here."

"We can always jump," Fareed says from a distance. "Broken legs are a small price to pay."

"Pleasant thought," Tomás murmurs. Gunshots sound again, closer, and he tenses. Then he pulls me to him. "None of this is your fault," he says into my hair. "You couldn't have stopped him even if you had talked to someone. I love you."

And I know, no matter how many secrets I may have, he'll always be there for me.

It makes me feel safe.

....

TOMÁS

I hope she smiles again. She's radiant when she smiles. Which isn't surprising. She has the same genes as me, of course. "I'm sorry we fought so much this past year. We wasted so much time. If I had known we'd end up here…"

She squeezes me tightly. "If you had known, we still would've fought. It's what we do best."

That's true. Of course it's true.

Twin brother privileges.

I draw out this moment for as long as I dare—Sylvia on

the window ledge, freedom at her back, and me standing in front of her. Time pauses long enough for me to tell her, "You know, you aren't the only one with secrets. I always wanted to study archaeology, like a modern Indiana Jones but slightly less racist. Focus on our own heritage. I always thought Abuelo would like that. Tell him, won't you?"

Maybe he'll understand, in the end.

"Tell Mamá... I—I don't even know. Tell her I picked the locks on the auditorium and that supergluing Mr. Herrera's desk was the best decision I ever made. Tell her about that time we spiked the milk in the cafeteria with food coloring so it all turned green. And how we hid chickens in the teachers' lounge. Tell her I asked the prettiest girl in the school out on a date today—and she didn't even say no." My voice swells as I help her out the window. She's listening so intently, she doesn't seem scared as Fareed lifts her down onto the roof.

I expect her to argue or to laugh at me, but her dark eyes are serious. And in that moment, I love her for being there.

"Hell, just tell Mamá I had a wonderful sister. Tell her I had the most amazing friends." The air outside is crisp, and I can almost taste the promise of snow. "Tell her I was happy, okay?" I smile. "Tell her I was happy, and don't let her forget me."

With those words, I let go of Sylv's hands. I hope she'll remember me smiling too. Sliding the window shut behind her, I turn away so I don't have to see her look of surprised betrayal when she realizes I'm not going with her. I take a calming breath, then walk back to the door. They need time—and time is what I can give them.

CJ Johnson
@CadetCJJ
The auditorium is almost empty while we're waiting to get out.
10:43 AM

272 favorites

CJ Johnson
@CadetCJJ
Someone will wake me up and tell me it was all a dream, right? #OHS
10:44 AM

Jay Eyck
@JEyck32
@CadetCJJ I wish #OHS
10:44 AM

CHAPTER TWENTY-ONE

CLAIRE

Nothing else matters but the silence on the other side of the line.

For Matt's sixth birthday, we pimped an old tricycle to make it look like a spaceship. Dad cut the parts from cardboard, and Trace and I painted them in whatever colors Matt wanted—red with streaks of blue, purple with green dots, black stripes and white stars. It didn't look like anything special, but Matt was overjoyed. That cardboard spaceship was the start of his obsession with anything with wings—to the point where Dad once said he and Mom would have to get him flying lessons instead of driving lessons. The mere thought of it had Matt bouncing around the house for days.

Chris hands me a paper cup of water, but I don't feel thirsty. I don't feel anything. Part of me waits for Matt to cough, to *breathe*, but I know it's futile. I know.

When Matt was twelve, we drove down to the coast

so he could see the ocean—well, the gulf. It was the only vacation we had gone on since he was born, but that summer was special. Dad had a new job. Tracy had enlisted and would leave for training in the fall.

We ate dinner first and walked along the beach at sunset, all of us helping Matt when his crutches got sucked into the muddy sand. By the time darkness shimmered across the water, we had sand in our shoes, our clothes, our hair, our ears. We lay on our backs and stared at the stars, which were starting to appear, and Trace and I each held on to one of Matt's hands. He told us all about the constellations overhead.

"I love that the sky is endless," he said. "If I can't go to space, I want to study the stars. Do you know the light we see really means we're looking back in history?"

"Does that mean we're in the future?" Trace laughed.

"No. We're at exactly the right place, at exactly the right time."

Today, I was at neither. When Chris gently switches off the phone, I stuff my hands in my pockets and start to pace. On the other side of the police tape, people wrap their arms around each other and cry, hold hands and pray, whisper words of encouragement to each other. There are so many people here, and Chris is by my side, but I have never felt more alone. I wish my parents were here, but at the same time I'm not ready to face them. Not yet. Maybe not ever.

When I spot Deputy Lee in the crowd, I touch his arm and draw him to a quiet spot. "How can we help?"

"You know that's not possible, Claire."

"Anything at all?"

The deputy shakes his head. We're victims too, with names and witness reports to be taken.

But I need to do *something*.

"Please."

He wavers, and I push. "Please. *Anything*." Anything to stop me from losing my mind. From feeling like I failed everyone.

When Chris takes my hand and echoes my words, Deputy Lee guides us to the large shelter. "If you want to help, talk to the students who are afraid. They would benefit from seeing familiar faces. Our officers will take their names and their reports. The most important thing you can do is be there."

A gesture of kindness. It's all we need.

"After the students are registered and checked for injuries, they will be escorted to an emergency center in town. There, they'll be reunited with their families as they arrive." He hesitates, as if unsure whether this is a good idea. "If at any point this becomes too much for you, you let us know and we'll make sure you get there too. You should be there to wait for your families."

"Opportunity High is our family," I say. "We can listen."

Chris reaches for my hand and squeezes. With everything that has happened, I don't know who I am.

I am a sister—was—*am*.

I hope.

A handful of students head our way, and I straighten despite my trembling hands. A girl breaks away from the group and walks toward me.

....

AUTUMN

When a handful of police officers lead a group of students out of the auditorium, I grab my chance. I trail them, at the back of the group, and shiver when we cross the threshold to the hallway. I take in the bullet holes in the lockers, more bodies and blood spatters on the linoleum.

And I hang back to get my bearings. *Where would Sylv go?* Maybe she's outside already. Maybe she's safe. In here, there are too many bodies, too many signs that Ty continued his rampage.

Where would Ty go? If he stayed on this floor or if he'd gone outside, the police would have captured him and the paramedics would be here already and we wouldn't need to sneak out.

It'd make most sense for him to go to the second floor.

My cut stings, and I wipe at my cheek with my sleeve,

which only makes the pain worse. I hang near the wall and let the group walk away from me. The soft static of the officers' radios fades.

I won't have much time.

Once the auditorium is clear, they'll do a sweep of the school, I think. As soon as the group turns the corner, I'll run to the staircase. I'll be careful. I'll be quiet. If Sylv is upstairs, so is Ty. I won't let either of them go without a fight. They're all I have left.

A shot rings out upstairs.

"We have to get you out," one of the officers says, hurrying the group along.

Everyone rushes toward the front of the school, to safety, protected on either side by the SWAT team. No one notices me.

Another shot sounds upstairs, and I make my way toward the second floor. In the dim lighting, the stairwell feels haunted—even more so when I see two students sprawled across the steps, their blank eyes staring at me.

Neither are Sylv.

We had planned to go to New York together. Not for my audition—I needed to do that on my own—but after that. If I got accepted. We were going to go after Sylv graduated, our own private road trip. A visit to Juilliard, then up to Brown—because of course she'll get in—and wherever else we wanted to go.

Away from here, we'd face the world. We'd build our home. Together.

Oh God. I hope I'm not too late.

....

TOMÁS

I quietly close the door behind me and move away from it. It'll be easy for Tyler to find the one that's unlocked, but it will take him time—time we have and he doesn't, because with every second, more students escape and the police move closer.

They have to. They have to save us.

Run, Sylvia, run.

I walk fast to get as far away from the room as possible. Across the hall, Tyler tries another door. Locked. When he turns, his gun in hand and an agitated look in his eyes, he spots me and pauses. He no longer looks neat and immaculate. There are blood spatters on his shirt, and his spiky hair is ruffled.

"You know, *sweaty chic* doesn't suit you," I muse.

Tyler falters, though only for a moment. "I should have known. Come to protect your sister? What are you going to do—hit me again?"

"I'll always protect her," I say. I thought I would have to struggle to keep my anger under control, but all I have to do is think about Sylvia and Fareed running, running, running. As long as they're safe, nothing else matters.

My calm seems to throw him off guard, but a slow grin spreads across his face. I can't imagine a more eerie reaction from someone holding a gun.

"You think you're something, don't you? The joker of the school," he says. "Are you afraid now? This time, I'm in control, and there is nothing you can do about it."

"You'll kill me. That's that. So no, I'm not afraid." I shrug while sweat runs down my back and my arms. "Funny thing though, that still means *I* am in control."

He pulls the trigger, and I flinch. The bullet buries itself in the wall beside me. Tyler's gloating makes me want to charge him. But I refuse to give him that pleasure.

"You'll kill me on my terms," I say, and I hate that my voice trips and breaks.

Firing his gun, on the other hand, seems to have made Tyler more confident. He takes a step closer and points the gun at my head. "At least you won't be in my way anymore. Was that your brilliant plan? Protect your sister by sacrificing yourself? Just imagine what I can do without you around to protect her."

"Nothing more than with me here." Inwardly, I wince at how true those words are. "You see, we have friends. I know it must be hard for you to understand, but I know she'll be safe, and she'll know she's loved. Whereas you—you're a maggot, and soon you'll be a dead maggot. I may be dead, but you won't hurt her anymore."

He raises an eyebrow. "Was telling me that worth it?"

I eye the barrel, and I can almost feel Sylvia's arms around me, see the look in her eyes whenever I made her laugh, whenever Autumn danced, whenever we were all together at the farm and Mamá was having one of her good days. I can't protect her from every danger, but I can give her more days to love.

Telling him wasn't worth it. But delaying him long enough for Sylv to escape?

"It's so worth it."

....

SYLV

No, no, no, no, no.

He can't—Tomás can't leave me.

On this side of the window, the sound of voices drifts up on the wind—parents, police, camera crews. Vehicles come and go. Helicopters rattle the air. It feels as though we've been dropped back into the real world, into *life*. On the other side of the roof, Fareed is signaling to the police, but I need Tomás with me.

Ragged sobs burst from my chest as I claw at the window. There are no handles from this side, and I'm not even sure if there's a way to open it, but that doesn't stop me from trying. I scratch at the window frame.

"Sylv." Fareed's strong hands guide mine away from the glass. He is so close, it makes me want to lash out, but he holds me while I struggle—against his hands, against the window, against everything that keeps me from my brother.

I struggle against his voice too. I won't listen. I don't want to hear what he has to say.

Fareed does not take that into account though. "Tomás knows what he's doing. He wanted—"

"Don't you dare," I cut him off. "Don't tell me what he wanted to do or that everything might be fine."

"He would not have wanted you to go back inside!"

"I can't stay out." I shake my head. I can't stop shaking my head. "I won't leave the classroom, I promise. But I can't stay here. I can't stay here."

I look down, and it's as if the ground twists and turns under my feet, as if the school is trying to shake us off. Fareed loosens his grip a little, and I sink to the roof. My arms shake. The shingles chafe my knees.

In front of us, a chopper circles, and someone in a black uniform calls to us. The noise distorts his words, and it's impossible to understand him.

I push further into myself while Fareed's hands fall away. He edges toward the helicopter, shouting back to the officer.

With Fareed distracted, I stand and try to push the window open again. We opened this. Tomás didn't lock it. I should be able to open it again. I *have to*. The vinyl of the frame is too smooth to give me a good grip, but the window gives way. An inch, just an inch.

Fareed turns to me and tries to stop me, but once my grip is solid, the rest is easy. I pull myself up and launch myself through the open window, escaping his grasp and diving headlong toward the floor.

I scramble to my feet and close the window to block the sound and Fareed when the silence stops me in my tracks. It's terrifying.

On the other side of the door, gunshots echo through the hallway.

One.

Two.

Three.

Tyler's unmistakable voice. "I win."

Jay Eyck
@JEyck32
No words for today. Mb there never will be.
#OHS
10:45 AM

Abby Smith
@YetAnotherASmith
@JEyck32 I'm so sorry. #OHS
10:45 AM

Family North
@FamNorthOpp
@JEyck32 We're praying for you. #OHS
10:45 AM

Father Williams
@SacredHeartOpportunity
@FamNorthOpp @JEyck32 We'll hold a
candle mass tonight. All are welcome.
10:45 AM

CHAPTER TWENTY-TWO

SYLV

A blanket of gray covers Opportunity. Tomás loved days like these. Even though he hated work on the farm, he loved going outside when the sky was overcast. When we still had horses, he would stay in the stables to sit out the storm; then he would saddle one of the mares and ride off as soon as the sky cleared, the thick smell of ozone still heavy in the air.

After Mamá's diagnosis, he wouldn't wait for the rain to clear. When we sold the horses, he'd go running as soon as the first drops of rain pelted the windows, and he'd come back soaking wet and happy.

Abuelo complained about it all the time. "He'll catch his death," he said. "He goes running toward it like an old friend, and it will embrace him before he knows."

Tomás always shrugged off these comments. "I'm running with the wind," he'd say. "And no one will ever catch me. Not even death."

I sag against the wall, and another bang shakes my memories. I tell myself that was all it was—thunder. A storm come to sweep him off his feet.

Come to make him fly.

....

CLAIRE

"I don't know where Rae is. She was sitting next to me when the doors opened, but when we ran, I lost track of her. Has she been here?" The girl in front of me trembles. Her blond hair is matted against her forehead.

The officer next to me flicks through pages of notes, but he comes up with nothing. "We have vans to take you to the emergency center in Opportunity. If she makes it out, you'll see her there."

"What do you mean 'if'?" Her voice cracks, but she is gently led away and another student gives his name with a steady voice.

"Steve Johnson." He has black hair, wears black clothes. Although Steve's a junior, he's in some of my classes. His little sister is on my drill team. I want to ask him about her, the determined, mousy-haired girl who became the backbone of our group. She planned to start a color guard troop on campus. We were supposed to have coffee this week to talk about organizing it.

I want to ask him about her, but I don't have to. Apparently, we all have the same questions in our eyes. *What have you seen? Who have you lost? What can you tell us?*

"I don't know where CJ is," he says quietly. He wipes at his eyes, leaving a smudge of black eyeliner on his cheeks before he's led to a van that will shuttle him to the center in Opportunity.

They keep on coming, students and the occasional teacher or staff member, each with their own stories of the lost and questions about the missing. And all we can do—all we must do—is listen and be supportive.

"I know she's still alive. She has to be. We were planning to go to Europe together this summer. Just us and our backpacks. London, Paris, Rome. We are going to visit Big Ben and picnic in front of the Eiffel Tower and see the Colosseum. She wanted to go to Berlin too. Her family is originally from Germany, you know? She wanted—"

"He shot him right in front of me. The bullet went through his neck. There was so much blood. Will you tell his parents? What did he want with us? What did we ever do to him?"

"I don't know where she is."

After another group of students leaves and we're left waiting, I sink into a chair. My heart is empty, and my head is full. The stories tumble over one another. We're grief counselors simply because we're *there*. I can understand why Deputy Lee did not want us here. I never realized that courage was so terrifying.

But even if the stories are horrific, everyone coming through our tent shares a common understanding.

It fills our emptiness.

Strong arms wrap themselves around me as Chris pulls me into a hug. His heartbeat thumps against my cheek. I place my hand on the nape of his neck, tracing his goose bumps. His hands trail from my shoulders to my ears as he pushes a strand of hair out of the way.

"You are so brave," Chris's voice rumbles, deep and low.

....

AUTUMN

This floor covers only a third of the school's first floor. Even so, the corridor feels like it goes on forever. The doors on either side of the hallway are closed. I stay close to the wall. Voices from downstairs float up, the clipped commands of freedom and safety, of SWAT officers filtering into the school.

This hallway seems untouched by the violence below. But on closer inspection, I see bullets have drilled themselves into wooden doors and the cinderblock walls.

At least here are no bodies. No Sylv. *I hope they made it to the roof.*

At the corner, I crouch low and peek around it. Ty stands in the center of the hallway, and he swings his gun wildly.

"You won't get in my way again," he rants. "You won't stop me from showing your sister her place. You are too late. Do you hear that? You've lost."

I inch closer to see who he's talking to, only to come to a full stop when the scene unfolds in front of me.

Tomás's prone body lies at Tyler's feet.

The Adventures of Mei

Current location: Opportunity High

>> Whenever we see survivors, there is a sparkle of hope. Maybe our friends, maybe our loved ones are coming too. If we hold hands, we can form a safety net for those who are still wandering and lost. Like when Mrs. Morales arrived with her father. She's rarely out in public anymore. There was such a frantic look in her eyes, but someone brought her tea, the colonel's wife came to stand next to her and whispered soothing words, and everyone formed a circle around her. Dad always cared so much about common humanity—that was why he became a teacher. I hope he found it inside. I think he'll find it here.

If he gets out—when he gets out.

Comments: <disabled>

CHAPTER TWENTY-THREE

AUTUMN

My breath catches. The sound startles Ty. He pivots to face me. "What are you doing here?" he demands.

The bitterness in his voice is palpable. I stare past him at Tomás, who lies on the ground. Ignoring the gun, I slide past my brother and crouch next to Tomás's body to close his unseeing eyes.

"There are SWAT teams downstairs," I say. "It's only a matter of time before they're here. It's over." *You lost*, I want to add, but I know better than that. It would only anger him more. Besides, if anyone lost, it's us. It's Opportunity. It's Sylv, who can't be far off if Tomás is—was—here. "Give it up, Tyler."

He doesn't respond, but at least he hasn't shot me yet.

The gun hangs useless by Ty's side. This time, however, I don't try to advance on him.

"You know, after Mom died, apart from Sylv, you were the only one to ever see me dance. You know the ballet shoe charm you bought me for my birthday last year?" I keep my eyes down as I show him the bracelet around my wrist, blood smudged on the silver. "I've never taken it off."

In the distance, the sound of boots—slow, careful, on the lookout for traps—comes from the stairs. Coming closer.

When Ty's hand brushes my wrist, my voice trips. "I planned to wear it to my audition. You were always with me. You are always with me. You never had to be alone, Ty."

....

CLAIRE

With the exodus of students comes more news of the dead.

The young officer sitting to the side of the tent records their names. We're not supposed to hear them. The report is part of the crime scene, and as long as the bodies haven't been retrieved and verified, their deaths are not official.

Though that will be of little comfort to the parents—or to Chris and me. We all hear the names and recognize too many of them.

A current passes through the crowd with the news of each survivor. Relief and sorrow follow each other rapidly, because with the names of those who live comes the void of those who have not. Death brings life; life brings death.

There are no words in that fleeting moment between hope and the knowledge. There is no way to express how a heart can burst and break at the same time, how the sun can cut through the darkness but will cast shadows everywhere.

There are only fingers that entwine with another's, arms that link in solidarity.

With every new name, someone breaks down and someone else holds them up. At the entrance to the student parking lot, police officers inform parents and families to report to Opportunity's church for further processing and possible questioning. But few of them leave. Instead they stay here, together. And even if they sought comfort elsewhere, we'd all know where to find whomever we needed. Opportunity is no place for secrets. Not anymore. Not after today.

We are home.

....

SYLV

Autumn's voice swirls around me, just out of reach. *SWAT teams upstairs. Police outside*, I repeat in my mind.

It's over.

It's over.

Madre de Dios, I hope she's right. But it's so, so

impossible to believe. With all that has happened, today won't be over. Today will never be over again.

If only Tomás had waited a few minutes longer—

Fareed slips in through the window, and I expect him to try to pull me out to the roof again.

I cradle my knees to my chest and shake my head.

His shoulders drop. Fareed sags down next to me against the wall. He wraps an arm around my shoulders, and I lean against him. We don't make a sound. I listen to Autumn try to reason with Tyler. *Please listen. Please end this.*

"Everyone I've loved," I whisper. "Everyone I love is slipping through my fingers."

Fareed bows his head. "For the first few weeks after we came here, my father would tell me the same thing every night: You can't always keep your loved ones with you. You can't always settle your life in one place. The world was made to change. But as long as you cherish the memories and make new ones along on the way, no matter where you are, you'll always be at home."

Jay Eyck
@JEyck32
I don't know what to do now. We're all waiting. #OHS

10:47 AM

134 favorites 150 retweets

CHAPTER TWENTY-FOUR

SYLV

Fareed reminds me of something Mamá once told me—
and that only makes the pain worse.

*When Autumn first began wearing Tyler's charm, the
only telltale sign that she was already working on an
application to Juilliard, she had a soft light in her eyes
and a faint blush on her cheeks. She was so proud of
it. She said it was the first real acknowledgment she'd
had since her mom died that someone understood what
dancing meant to her, and it mocked me. I remember
running home from school that day, needing space to
be by myself. Mamá sat on the porch outside. She'd
made tea for the both of us, and although it was black
enough to be coffee and the cookies she dug up were
stale, she smiled.*

"How was school, niña?"

*Seeing her matted curls around her face and her hands
sitting calmly on her lap, I forgot about the charm and*

Tyler. Instead, I dropped my bag and sat down on the porch next to her.

"School was good, Mamá," I said. "I sent in my college application."

"I'm so proud of you." She always said that even though her lucid days were few and far between. "You and your brothers, you'll make something of your lives."

She didn't protest when my brothers came home to care for her, all of us taking turns, but she took notice. And she cared that Tomás and I went to college more than any of us, especially these last few months.

I nibbled on a chocolate chip cookie. "Yes, Mamá."

"Just don't forget where you came from. Don't forget the stories of our family."

"No, Mamá." My replies came automatically because I wanted her to keep talking. We didn't need to have deep and meaningful conversations. It was special to simply sit with her and talk about the mundane things—school, homework, the future.

But she was perceptive that day, and she raised an eyebrow. "Don't take that tone with me, young lady." Then she laughed, the sound all throaty and warm. She laughed as if it were the funniest thing in the world. Giggles rose in my chest until I couldn't hold on to them any longer, and I snorted out my tea, hiccupping and laughing at the same time.

"No, Mamá."

That set her off all over again. Abuelo pulled up the driveway and sat there in the truck, his window rolled down, staring at us as if we'd both gone mad. We couldn't stop laughing. And it healed a rift between us, all the words unspoken and forgotten.

A few minutes after Abuelo went into the house, Mamá stilled. "I'll miss you, my wonderful daughter. I wish I could stay with you forever, to see you grow into the woman I always knew you would be. You are so strong, but promise me you will take care of your brothers."

I laid my head on her lap, and she stroked my hair. I promised, "Always, Mamá."

Always.

"Far?" I sit up, although I don't meet his eyes. "How do I explain to Mamá that Tomás isn't coming home?"

He doesn't have an answer to that. Neither do I.

·······

CLAIRE

Although the idea of setting up an emergency center where students and families can be reunited is good in theory, it turns out to be mostly impractical, as those students pass their families to get to the main road.

Many are intercepted—and reunited—before they

even reach the vans. There is nothing better than seeing smiles and happy tears, especially when SWAT officers return with another group of students. They signal that more students are on their way, not far behind, and wild hope whispers through the crowd. Part of me is still waiting for Matt to walk out too.

Except for every student present, the ghost of another student haunts us. With every tally mark, the dead creep closer.

"Sarge!"

A voice rises above the others and makes my heart jump. Leading a group of the rescued students is CJ.

"You don't know how often I've wished to be a tracky today," she says as she wraps her arms around me. She tries to make light of it, but there's a trace of bitterness. I can't imagine all she's seen.

She stands tall. Her hair is still neatly braided, her clothes impeccable, but her eyeliner is running. And with every word she speaks, her mood grows darker. "I wish I had one of our drill guns. I could have knocked him out. Or at least I could have tried. I should have—I'm so sorry—" Fierce, unbreakable CJ breaks. "All those deaths. How could it happen here? Why couldn't we stop it?"

I don't have an answer, but I reach out to take her hand. "If you could have done anything, I know you would have. Steve is looking for you. He's at the shelter."

Her whole face lights up. Then she starts sobbing. I pull her close, smoothing her hair and holding her while her shoulders shake.

"It'll be all right," I say softly. "You're both safe now. You're both alive and you're both safe."

She looks up at me, her face tearstained. "I—I watched his friends die."

....

AUTUMN

"I love you, you know. I only wanted us to be a family. That's all I ever asked of you," I say.

Ty uses the gun to push a wayward strand of hair out of his face. He's sweating so hard, the gel won't hold. With his free hand, he polishes the blood off the bracelet.

"It's all I ever asked of you too," he says. His voice is calm, and the madness fades in his eyes. "We should have been there for each other."

He releases my wrist, and my knees give way. I slide down the wall to sit next to Tomás's body.

Ty sticks the gun into his waistband and takes off his blazer. He jerks his head in Tomás's direction before he pins me with a stare. "The world is against us. You need to understand that before it kills you."

It's rich, coming from the kid with the gun. But his

monotone leaves me far more afraid than his raging ever did.

"Give in, Ty," I try. "There is nothing left to gain from shooting anyone."

"No, there isn't," he says. He neatly folds the jacket and places it on the floor. He retrieves his gun and sits down in front of me.

The footsteps and voices have reached our floor. The officers are still too distant to hear what's being said, but they're moving with more confidence now.

"You won't kill me." A hint of panic creeps into my voice. "We're family. That must count for something."

"It does." He takes off his watch and stares at it. I wonder how much time has passed. Minutes. An hour maybe. It feels like days, an eternity. It's impossible to imagine the world around us has continued its normal rhythm. Ty folds the watch and puts it into his pocket. "Our family was everything to me once."

"It's everything to me too." There are so many things I would have done differently if I had the chance.

Ty stares at me. I want to scramble to my feet, get away while I still can, but the barrel of his gun tells me to stay. "Who will mourn you, Autumn?"

His question and my answer leave me numb. Apart from Sylv, *no one will mourn me*.

I stand. "The police will be here at any moment.

This'll be the end of it, and you will have accomplished nothing."

He stares at me over the barrel, and the corner of his mouth twitches. A smirk. Then a smile—a smile full of delight and mischief.

When he pulls the trigger, I feel the shot rather than hear it. Pain overwhelms me. The floor opens up around me. The last thing I see before I fade is Ty turning the gun on himself. The last thing I hear is Ty saying, "I just don't want to be alone anymore."

Then he blows his brains out.

CJ Johnson

@CadetCJJ

The daylight is too bright here at #OHS

10:49 AM

CJ Johnson

@CadetCJJ

I hate this world sometimes.

10:49 AM

CJ Johnson

@CadetCJJ

But my brother is alive. We're lucky.

10:50 AM

CHAPTER TWENTY-FIVE

SYLV

At the sound of the shots, I shiver and curl up. The door slams open against the wall, and I scream. I *scream*, but Fareed pulls me in and smothers the sound. The smell of blood and smoke is overwhelming.

Three police officers barge in, weapons at the ready, shouting for us to raise our hands.

Fareed slowly releases me and follows instructions. One of the officers raises the visor of his helmet, but he doesn't put down the gun.

"Are you armed?"

"No, sir," Fareed says.

I merely shake my head.

"How did you get here?"

"We opened the door of the auditorium," Fareed says. "My friend and I. I was the one who called 911 from the principal's office." He continues, but the words sweep past me. I was there—I don't need to relive it.

I glance at the doorway. The other two officers have completed their sweep of the room and seem satisfied. Sounds filter in from the hallway. And with every set of footsteps, my heart soars and drops. Maybe Fareed was right—maybe Tomás did know what he was doing. Maybe I imagined the gunfire. It won't be the first time I underestimated my brother; he's always had a knack for getting away with anything.

Someone knocks on the door.

I nearly jump out of my skin.

"Miss." One of the officers kneels down in front of me and places what is surely meant to be a comforting hand on my shoulder. My skin crawls and I shudder, shaking him off.

"Don't. Don't touch me."

Fareed quickly says, "Sylv, it's the police. It's okay."

The officers talk with each other before one turns and disappears again.

"We'll get you out of here." The officer rocks to his feet, and Fareed scrambles to help me stand.

With two officers flanking us, we head toward the hallway. My heart trips when we cross the threshold.

Fareed's hand squeezes mine.

Away from the windows, the light is dimmer. And perhaps it would be better not to see at all. Perhaps it would be easier not to see what we've lost.

I blink.

Tomás is slumped against the wall. My knees weaken, and my stomach revolts.

Tomás.

Brother.

Tyler is sprawled opposite him. His face is destroyed. And if I expected to feel victorious, I am mistaken. Here, at the broken places, all I feel is emptiness.

A few steps away, Autumn lies curled and shaking. I break out in sobs. Officers surround her, and one of them kneels beside her, trying to draw her attention. She doesn't respond. She twists and turns and pushes them away from her. Her fingers are curled around Tyler's hand. Her face is white. The linoleum around her is stained red.

She came for us. For her brother. For me.

She came for us after all.

....

CLAIRE

One of the officers guides CJ toward the vans that will take her to Opportunity, to Steve. Chris steers me to a black girl standing to the side of the tent. Her lips are set in an angry line, and she keeps clasping and unclasping her hands in front of her. I only know she's a fellow senior because we had English together sophomore year, but other than that, we've managed to pass each other for four years.

"My sister was in your brother's class. They got along well." She spits out the words. "Your boyfriend killed her. He shot your brother too."

Suspecting it, knowing it, is still not the same as having it confirmed. There's no pretending now. I waver. The only thing that keeps me standing is Chris's hand supporting my elbow.

"I think he got shot accidentally. He couldn't walk. When we were rushed out, they left him behind." She stares at me, her eyes as fierce as the colors in her hair, but her voice dips. "I think they were too late."

"I'm sorry for your loss" is all I can manage.

She takes a shaky breath. "I'm sorry for yours."

The words don't make sense, but I nod. She disappears into the blur of faces. Chris is the only one whose presence registers, and I collapse.

"Let me know as soon as you hear anything about the scholarships. I don't care if it's the middle of the night. I'm so proud of you." Tracy stood outside the base, one hand on my shoulder.

She looked untouchable in her immaculate uniform, her lieutenant's bars polished to a shine. Her eyes sparkled, and even her hair looked perfect. I wanted to be her. We hugged, and I whispered, "Are you scared?"

She laughed. "I'm terrified."

"Oh good, me too."

"You'll be just fine. Take care of Matt, okay? You're the eldest now. Opportunity High will be rough for him, at least the first couple of months. But tell him it's okay to be scared. We all are. It's part of growing up."

Chris reaches for my hand, and all I want to do is wrap my arms around him and cling to him, to know that at least there is one part of my life that is strong and safe.

I hate myself for wanting to be happy.

"Are you—" Chris swallows the question. "Stupid question. I'm sorry."

I weave my fingers around his. "Are you—?"

He shakes his head. "No, I'm not."

"Me neither." I pause. "But I'm glad you're here."

Chris braves a wan smile. "I will always be here."

"I know," I say, and to my surprise, I do. Today leaves us with so many questions. Of all the people who died here today, did anyone really know anyone else? What they feared? What they wished for? Who they wanted to be?

But this I do know: Chris will always be there when I need him.

"I don't want to be alone anymore."

Things changed between us. We need to figure out who we want to be, who we can be, who we are. "I want to teach," I blurt out.

267

Chris shakes his head and starts to laugh. The sound is strange amid all the grief, but it is also beautiful and healing.

A white girl runs in. I've seen her around the hallways, though I don't know her name. She is crying just like all of us, but when she stands in the middle of our tent, everyone stops what they're doing to listen.

"He's dead. He shot himself. I overheard it on the radio." She turns to the officer near the tent opening. He shakes his head apologetically. He can't say anything. But she can. And she does.

"It's over."

....

AUTUMN

There is nothing left but pain. Flashes of life and flashes of intense darkness. Noise. Everything hurts.

When I close my eyes, Ty's half smile taunts me. *When Ty pointed the gun at me, he smiled like he did when Mom brought home chocolate oranges from the UK. I wanted to see him happy for so long. But then he pulled the trigger.*

When I open my eyes, I'm trapped in an endless pirouette, as if someone gave me a spin and I can't stop. The linoleum feels cool under my cheek. All I want to do is let go.

"Miss."

A face hovers over me.

"Miss, can you hear me?"

A thousand knives stab my leg. All the screaming makes me feel sick.

"We need a paramedic, stat."

They won't come, I think, because I can still see Matt lying in the auditorium. They won't come. They will never come. *Save those who will survive the rescue. Start there.*

But the danger has passed. We *are* safe.

If that's true, why don't I feel safe? Why can't I move? Why is someone screaming until my throat's sore? Am I screaming?

Someone tries to move me, but I jerk back.

"What's her name?" someone asks.

"Autumn," a familiar voice answers. "Autumn Browne."

Sylv.

"Autumn?" It's the first voice again, soothing and reassuring. "We'll try to make you more comfortable, but we need to move you. We're going to stabilize your leg first."

My leg? I nod, but when I try to raise my hands to meet Sylv's, they don't move. I'm not sure they ever did.

"Golondrina."

Hot tears fall on my face while cool hands fold against my forehead. They draw me out of my nightmares. I open my eyes, and the colors swim. "Sylv..." I say it again to make sure my mouth forms her name right, but she doesn't respond. She caresses my cheek.

She takes my hand in hers because I still do not remember how to move. She presses her lips to my fingers, and I want to hold her—no matter who might see.

She glances down at my legs. Her pity and helplessness are so clear.

I wanted to dance so much, it tore me up inside. I was willing to sacrifice everything to dance. But when Ty pointed the gun at me, he broke me. I'll never mend again.

Ty made good on his promise. I didn't need to die for him to kill me. He simply lowered his gun and pulled the trigger. And his bullet tore my knee to shreds.

Jay (@JEyck32) ➜ Kevin (@KeviiinDR)

Ill be waiting. Ill be waiting until Im able to say goodbye to you. Or maybe, maybe, maybe hello.

10:53 AM

Jay (@JEyck32) ➜ Kevin (@KeviiinDR)

I wish I knew how little time we had.

10:53 AM

CHAPTER TWENTY-SIX

SYLV

I hold Autumn's hand as the paramedics get her onto a stretcher, as they carry her toward the stairs. The SWAT teams lead us out, but they leave Tyler and Tomás behind. It's so wrong, seeing them there together—together and yet so, so far apart.

A smile plays around Tomás's lips.

Something inside me waits for him to stand up and follow us out.

But he doesn't.

Autumn moans. She's clear some moments, only to fade away the next. Her leg is a bloody mess, and I don't know how they'll be able to fix it. I don't know how she'll ever dance—how she'll ever soar through the air again.

I wanted to keep her. I wanted to be her home. I wanted her to fly, but I always hoped she would come back to me.

Not like this though. Never like this.

When we reach the first floor, the hallways are empty.

There are only the bodies and the bloodstains and the screams that haunt the school. On our way to the main entrance, we pass the doors to the auditorium, which are wide open now. The seats are empty. Paramedics care for the wounded, and policemen and detectives scour the area for evidence.

From this perspective, with the locks cut and all the doors open, the auditorium looks smaller. On any other day, the doors would open to laughter and discussions about our break. The doors would open, and we would head to our lockers, to Spanish, to my APUSH midterm. The doors would open to life.

The bell rings, signaling the end of third period.

Autumn groans on the stretcher. Her eyes flicker open. "Are we leaving? Are we free?"

I squeeze her hand. I want to kiss her, tell her I'm so sorry, that this is not how I meant to keep her.

Instead, I nod and blink against the sunlight as we emerge outdoors.

This is where we leave Opportunity behind.

....

CLAIRE

The voices of families and news crews, the sirens driving on and off the campus—it all fades to the background.

When the first ambulances carry the wounded away from the school, the crowds step aside to let them pass. The students on the field watch the school's main entrance in silence, motionless. Word has spread, even if it's not official yet. Relief overtakes the grief.

It is over.

I zigzag around the tents and the police units, staying to the side of the parking lot. Once I've passed the south side of the school, the police presence diminishes.

The farther I am from the command center, the fewer police cars there are. I duck under the plastic tape. On this side of the parking lot, it's all student cars. I remember all those times Tracy drove here to watch me run track. I remember all the times we would drive around, the top down on her old convertible, me in the front and Matt in the back, the wind playing with our hair so it felt like we were flying.

I head toward the woods behind the school. There is the constant flashing of the emergency lights, but only the birds give their occasional commentary here. No one stops me. The barren trees are dark. Matt always told me the woods here are haunted. He plans—he planned to take us on a ghost hunt someday. All of us.

God, I should call my sister. I should tell her.

I should go home.

In the distance, someone calls my name, and sirens tear through the silence again.

I rest my head in my hands and I cry.

....

AUTUMN

It's cold outside. The paramedics on either side of my stretcher carry me out with brusque efficiency while Sylv keeps hold of my hand. I drift in and out of consciousness. It's merciful, because in those instants, I do not have to wonder who I am, who I am supposed to be.

I do not want to see this world yet—this world Ty created and then left. This morning, I wished I could escape to anywhere, be anything. Now all my dreams are out of reach, and I wonder if I'll ever make it home again.

But Sylv is still beside me. I don't want to ever let her go. For all that we lost, we have gained each other. Maybe that's all we need for now.

This is our moment.

Sylv is with me as we pass the crowd of parents and police officers and news crews and survivors. She is with me as the paramedics carry me to an ambulance. She is with me.

Ty will still win if we give up now. If we live in fear. If we let go of ourselves and each other. So I will hold on to

Sylv's hand for as long as I can. Together, we can rebuild our dreams.

Sylv bends forward to kiss my hair. I reach for her, and my lips meet hers. In one kiss, I try to tell her everything I can't say yet. That I'm sorry, so sorry. That there are so many things I have to figure out. Who I was or who I can be. But that my heart is hers. And if she'll accept me, it's the best I can give us. We may not have forever.

But we still have tomorrow.

When she breaks away, big, fluffy snowflakes begin to drift down. And we are in orbit around each other.

The Adventures of Mei

Current location: Home, waiting

>> I've read the tweets and posts online. I know teachers died. I know what people say about Dad. But he taught me to read the hope between the lines. So I won't believe them. Not yet.

Dad always told me there are more stories in the universe than stars in the sky. And in every story, there's the light of hope. That's why the seniors sent lanterns up to the sky—to make sure the darkness is never absolute.

Comments: <disabled>

EPILOGUE

SYLV

Fareed broke into the school tonight. After it was cordoned off and the officers retired for the night, he sneaked in through the roof—the same way we tried to get out and didn't, but this time, he was prepared.

When he crawled out of the school again, he texted most of the senior class, and we spread the news through brothers and sisters, friends, neighbors, acquaintances. Not one us slept—not one of us could. So in the middle of the night, we found our way to Opportunity. In cars, on bikes, by foot. We picked up everyone who didn't have transportation.

It could be any other first day of the semester, the way the cars converge on the road to the school. The way the students stream out. The moon shines bright in the clear night sky, lighting up the field around us.

All of us.

Students and teachers. Opportunity.

But we aren't complete. When we reach out to join hands, we're all aware of the thirty-nine dead. Of the twenty-five in the hospital.

So many lost. So many broken.

Autumn is having surgery on her leg. She won't go to Juilliard for her audition. She might not dance again or she might work hard and heal and try again next year. Her dad won't stop her now. He'll never touch her again.

My Autumn would fight to dance, but after today, I don't know anymore.

The road has tripped her up, like it has us all. We don't belong to the rich, good earth, and we don't belong to the horizons.

We are tied to Opportunity, and maybe that's the way it's supposed to be. We plant our seeds here to take root and blossom.

Fareed stands on my left and squeezes my fingers so tight. His lips move in silent prayer. I open my mouth and close it again. I don't know what to say. I simply watch as our circle grows and more prayers are offered into the night. Someone brought candles, and we all take one. We take them for the missing too.

I reach out, and for the briefest, most heartbreaking moment, I expect Tomás's callused hands to wrap around mine and his thumb to tickle my palm. I expect him to reach over and tug at my hair and whisper, "Let's hide the candles."

I'd elbow him and hiss at him to not to be such an idiot.

Ah, Dios, I'd give anything to call him an idiot one more time.

The hand that meets mine is slender and strong. The girl beside me glances my way. A girl who once stood up for me at junior prom, when all this started. Or perhaps it started long before then.

Claire smiles politely. Her eyes are haunted by the loss of a brother too.

It's a new kinship between us.

Silence falls as the prayers cease, and all eyes turn to Fareed.

He speaks, his accent coloring his words. "We are not better because we survived. We are not brighter or more deserving. We are not stronger. But we are here. We are here, and this day will never leave us. Nor should it. We will remember the wounded. We will remember the lost."

He walks to the center of the circle where his bounty waits for us. More than three dozen lanterns are spread out over the grass. It's not time for the Lantern Festival yet. No bonfire, no marshmallows, no stories to tell.

Only this story of the thirty-nine we lost. With every name Fareed reads, a student steps forward and picks up a lantern. When the name of a teacher is called, other

teachers follow our lead. Near the end of our list—
"Matt"—my neighbor retrieves a lantern.

When Tomás's name is called, so do I.

I return to the circle and offer Fareed a wrinkled letter,
tightly rolled, to use as a fuse, to burn with the memory of
today. He smiles softly as he lights it. "We will remember
the thirty-nine tonight. We will remember them tomorrow. We will remember them for all our tomorrows. And
there will be many tomorrows; there'll be thousands of
them. So let's make them good ones. *We* are Opportunity,
and we will not be afraid. We are Opportunity, and we
will *live*."

The paper smolders, but it's enough to light the fuses.
Other sparks light up the darkness. The lanterns get lit one
by one. Slowly, the words on the paper lanterns become
visible. Mr. Jameson always asked the seniors to write
their hopes and dreams on the fragile paper. These are not
wishes but names.

I stare at Tomás's name as my vision swims with tears.
For a few precious seconds, I'm alone with my lantern
and my brother.

The lantern gently tugs upward. It's warm enough,
ready to be released. I hold on for one more moment.
Then, around me, other lanterns are released. They float
over our heads into the darkness, toward the promise of
a new day.

I take a deep breath and caress the rice paper between thumb and finger.

And I let go.

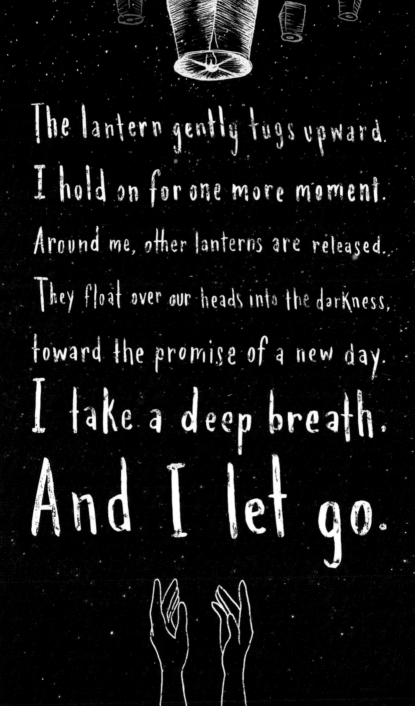

The lantern gently tugs upward.

I hold on for one more moment.

Around me, other lanterns are released.

They float over our heads into the darkness,

toward the promise of a new day.

I take a deep breath.

And I let go.

TURN THE PAGE FOR MORE
EXCLUSIVE CONTENT,

including a conversation with the author

AND

never-before-seen chapters of

this is where it ends

A LETTER FROM THE AUTHOR

My liberal arts high school was built out of particleboard and good intentions. It was meant to be a temporary building, but instead it stood for forty years. It was a good place—rickety, full of heart. The walls were painted in the brightest colors. My friends there were each creative in their own ways, and we had so many stories among us.

It wasn't a perfect time. There was heartbreak, as well as laughter, loss, and hopes and dreams. But—and I know what a privilege this was—my school felt relatively safe. It felt like a place where I could be who I was and pursue who and what I wanted to be. I'd known bullies and being bullied, but rarely there. I struggled with accessibility at other schools, but rarely there.

The scariest things we faced were economics midterms, German lit teachers, and the stability of the walls. Occasionally, we'd sit in class and see the rest of the school filter out in a fire drill that we were blissfully unaware of because the fire alarms didn't sound on our side of the school. Some days, we'd climb out of the windows and trade math for sing-alongs on the track field.

I didn't have to be afraid there.

Many years later, when I was in the United States for the first time, I thought about those high school experiences again. I was with a friend, and we were on our way to lunch when we passed a school bus.

I told my friend that back home, while some of us would get to school using public transportation, most of us would bike. We were—and are—very Dutch that way. I had classmates from surrounding towns and villages who might take an hour or more to get to school. Still, they would bike.

She asked a question.

I responded with one of my own.

That first conversation about the differences in our countries' school transportation evolved into a longer conversation about differences in school life and the high school experience. It was so interesting to discover that some experiences were entirely recognizable and relatable across oceans. (Though I would hesitate to call those experiences universal, because universality is too easy a way to erase individuality.)

We both spoke to how being a teen isn't easy, all the more so when you live along one or more axes of marginalization. We both understood high school as a period of friendship and choices and change—so much change.

We also talked about the intensity of high school, because, let's be honest, whether you have good experiences

287

or bad or—for most of us—a combination thereof, high school is a *lot*. It's like getting a bag full of puzzle pieces, but no one knows what the puzzle should look like or if the set is even complete.

Even now, some things I expected to have figured out by the time I graduated, I still haven't figured out. And that's perfectly okay. Our lives are constantly in motion, as is the world around us, and our stories are still being written.

But some high school experiences my American friend and I didn't share, and those parts of our conversation felt like talking across a chasm.

Back home, we experience violence at schools. Too much so. But lethal violence is rare, and school shootings are fairly nonexistent.

So I didn't understand.

I didn't understand how the possibility of death and fear of violence could be an almost accepted part of education. I knew and know it's not always avoidable. I lived with death for a long time, and I understand the fear of violence well. But I wondered: Could this not be avoided? Should this not be avoided?

I *wanted* to understand. I wanted to understand what it meant to live with that fear and live through that experience. And that set me on a journey that led to writing *This Is Where It Ends*.

I reached for books because that's what I do when I

have questions about the world. It started me on a path toward a lot of research. A lot of research.

I reached for stories, and stories reached for me. I found four characters who took up residency in my head. Four characters through whom I could explore all the questions I had, whose voices I couldn't shake. I wanted to follow them.

That led me to more research: To reading thousands of pages of nonfiction and reports. To meeting people and listening to their experiences. To asking more questions. To holding the weight of a gun.

It also lead me to take ballet with one of my best friends. To research track and field. To remember relatives with Alzheimer's. To figure out what *home* meant for someone who is still looking for one.

Because even a fictional disaster isn't merely a snapshot of one moment in one character's life. It's a lifetime. It's a web of moments, of communities, of families.

I knew if I wanted to write a story to explore all the questions I had, I needed to write the entire story. And meeting Sylv, Autumn, Tomás, and Claire gave me different lives to explore. I got to know them closely. I got to know their friends and families and their school, where they felt both other and at home. They had entire lifetimes to learn.

Opportunity High School was its own character too.

I had blueprints, a history of the building, and crafted far more detail about this place than a fictional school likely needs. It was built with paper and questions and inspiration.

But every now and then, while writing, editing, or reading, I found that I superimposed my particleboard school on top of it. My fictional high school and my own high school were at once entirely different and alike in many ways. They were full of heartbreak as well as laughter, loss, and hopes and dreams. The lockers changed color, the walls were brighter, and the linoleum became more worn.

I imagined.

Yet, I still didn't understand. Because I couldn't understand. I'd never been there. I had never shared that particular fear. But I could empathize. Isn't that what fiction teaches us as readers? In this world between words, we can be the best versions of ourselves. We can imagine and empathize fiercely.

I could ask questions and listen. In the safety of fiction, I could share my questions and Claire's questions and Sylv's questions and Tomás's questions and Autumn's questions, along with so many others who might bring their own questions to reading the book.

And I could hope. Not for snapshots, but for lifetimes. Lifetimes to explore. Lifetimes to live.

Because even if we never reach understanding, we can keep trying. Even if we never find definitive answers, we can keep asking. Because questions are where conversations start.

And questions are where stories start.

Marieke

PREQUEL

TOMÁS

The cafeteria is deserted. The hallways are deserted. The entire school is deserted except for Neil, the janitor, who stayed late to lock up. When he saw me, he merely sighed and looked away. But he's probably on the other side of the school somewhere, and the emptiness is eerie. After all, my sister isn't here.

This was our plan, mine and my sister's, for the first day of senior year—defy time and keep summer going for a few hours longer—but Sylv isn't coming. She changed after Mamá fell ill. She withdrew, from me and from everyone. She's become so quiet that she's almost disappeared, and a wall has grown between us that was never there before.

Her absence feels like pain.

And this is all I can do to break through that distance. To cheer her up and start the new school year on a sunny note.

Footsteps echo outside the cafeteria, followed by a muffled curse.

"C'mon, man. Open up."

I drop the bag of sand I'm carrying on the floor with a dull thud and rush to help. I brace to hold the heavy-duty doors open, while my willing accomplice staggers in, carrying a massive cardboard box full of deflated beach balls and other plastic items.

Before, it had always been Sylv and me against the world. We'd never needed anyone else. So I thought I would have to transform the school alone, which would've taken me far more than a few spare hours on the last afternoon before school starts after everyone's left the building to prepare for the first day. But serendipity led me to the perfect partner-in-pranks. The new kid in town, who seemed so careful when he transferred here during junior year, but who turned out to be open to the wildest plans, right when I needed him most.

Fareed.

He places the box of inflatables on one of the cafeteria tables and looks at me. "I hope you remembered to bring a pump."

I gape. "I thought you were bringing the pump! It'll take us forever to inflate everything!"

"Well, you should've..." Fareed trails off. He narrows his eyes, probably staring at the pump on the table behind me. He sighs in disgust. "You are the worst."

I smirk.

His mother's job moved him to Opportunity, of all places. I wouldn't wish that on my worst enemy, but I'm glad he's here, and I'm glad we both ended up at the church-slash-neighborhood barbecue that Granddad insisted my sis and I attend. Far looked as lost as we felt, and the three of us ducked out as soon as we politely could. Sylv went home, like she did most nights, but unlike most nights, she didn't leave me on my own. She left me with Far, at the edge of Opportunity, and during these summer weeks, he became the best friend I never had. He took to my terrible and wonderful plans with a vengeance. After all, he'd said, there is nothing quite like redecorating the cafeteria to make a name for yourself.

He pushes past me now. He picks up the pump and goes to work, while I go back to lugging around the heavy sandbags, spreading sand across the linoleum floor, until my arms ache.

"Will we get in trouble for this?" Far asks when, after another hour and a half, we both take a much-needed break.

"If they find out it's us? Oh, for sure." One of the reasons I like Fareed is that he's only just now considering the consequences of our prank. He agreed to my outrageous plan without worrying about getting caught or starting the year on the wrong foot. And, even now, he doesn't seem too fussed.

"I don't think Trenton will believe you were a part of it though. But me? I'd be in for it. Still, isn't that the point of a grand gesture?" I say, "I want my sister to know that this year is going to be *our* year. Bright, sunny, carefree." I want her to know I'll be there for her.

I just hope this makeshift beach lives up to what she wanted it to be.

And I hope the year *will* be better. At least that maggot Tyler, who'd been bothering her all throughout junior year, will be gone. Dropped out of school. Maybe she'll feel a little more at ease without him around. It'd be a step in the right direction, at least. I want my sister back.

Fareed kicks an inflated beach ball into the room. "Ballsy."

I groan at the terrible, terrible pun. "I have a reputation to live up to and the family name to uphold."

I've already told Fareed about that time my brother spray-painted the principal's car, and that time Sylv and I spiked the milk in the cafeteria. Turned it bright green. Harmless, but hilarious.

This time, it's Fareed who grins. "Such a noble mission."

"You jumped at the chance to help. Don't try to deny it."

"Well," he says, "you may have a reputation to uphold, but I have one to build. And there's no better time than the present, right?"

Fareed gestures at the sand strewn on the floor, the

inflatable palm trees leaning against the walls, the now-inflated dolphins that lay mixed in with fake plastic shells on the tables, and the beach balls in between the chairs.

Fareed produces a bright-orange starfish from the bottom of the box, all fake and glittery. With a frown, he places the kitschy thing on the center table, turning it this way and that until he's apparently satisfied. "It's all in the details, you know," he says with a grin.

Maybe it's because we've spent the last three hours changing the cafeteria into a beach oasis, but we both start laughing at the absurdity of the situation. And we can't stop.

"Far," I hiccup after a couple of minutes, "I think this is the beginning of a beautiful friendship."

More than that, this is going to be a wonderful school year, for all of us. Our senior year. Our last year. After that, Sylv will leave Opportunity the first chance she has, especially if she wants to follow Autumn. And Fareed will be off to college, no doubt. Hell, I might even talk Granddad into my plans, if I can muster up the courage. But for now, the three of us, we're here, and that's what counts. We're together, and we have a full school year ahead of us, a blank canvas for pranks and memories. We'll make sure we're remembered.

BONUS CHAPTER

JAY

Despite my best intentions to get up early, I wake up to daylight. Eagle, our tabby cat, sits next to me on my pillow, purring loudly. When I glare at her, she blinks.

My head *pounds*.

The house is quiet. Mom will kill me if she finds out I skipped school, but she has meetings in Birmingham all day, which means she left before six, and she won't be home until late. Plenty of time to get rid of this hangover.

I glance at the clock. 9:27 a.m. Assembly.

Shit. Coach will kill me too, when he realizes I'm not there. "You're a senior now, Jay," he'll tell me. "A football player whom the younger boys look up to. It's not just about what you do on the field; you have to set a good example off the field, as well."

Shit.

I sit up, and Eagle jumps off the bed with an angry yelp.

"Sorry, kitten," I mutter.

My vision twists, and I hold on to the edge of the bed to steady myself. Some role model I am.

I rarely drink more than a few glasses of beer and never on school nights. But last night saw the bottom of a bottle of tequila and I can't even remember how I got into bed. What was I *thinking*?

The answer to that, at least, is easy. I was thinking about Kevin. I'm always thinking about Kev these days, and I don't know what to do about it. He's been my closest friend since freshman year, but that friendship changed. And I don't quite understand it, but our relationship is different. New.

It scares me more than I want to admit.

He's not my first crush. I've had girlfriends. I've had crushes. I had a fling with a running back on one of the opposing teams at a tournament last summer. Most of the OHS team knows I'm bisexual, even though the rest of the school doesn't. I'm not worried about coming out, if that's what it takes to be with him.

But Kev knows me in a way that none of the others do—and I, him. When Mom and Dad split up and my sister moved away, he was there for me. When Coach threatened to kick me off the team after I flunked most of my classes, he helped me get back on track. When he snuck out of the house to go to his first Pride, I drove him to Birmingham. When he sent his first short story to a literary magazine, he used my laptop. He came to me when that maggot Tyler bullied him. Together, we set fire to Ty's locker in retaliation, and afterward we laughed and raged and got drunk.

We were friends, we *are* friends, but friends also became something more.

Kev effortlessly got under my skin, and I don't know that I'm ready for all that comes with that.

I'm not ready to start the day, either, but at 9:45 a.m. I still have a chance to salvage some of this day, before Coach notices I'm gone.

When the floor feels more steady under my feet, I get dressed with a grumble. My mouth tastes as if I chewed on a dead rat, and half a tube of toothpaste doesn't mask that. I need caffeine. And I need food. Large, quantities of greasy food. Fried chicken. Hash browns. Anything.

But even my hangover craving is tangled up with Kevin. The last time we got drunk together, we crashed here. We didn't *sleep* together, because that would be a terrible decision to make with the amount of alcohol we had, but we had breakfast together. We went out to get fries and burgers. And I could stop thinking about how right it felt to wake up next to him. It scares me endlessly to have him close. But what scares me more is fucking it up—our friendship, our...*more*. Losing him.

I head to the fridge to dig out cold, leftover pizza for breakfast. Eagle has forgiven me for dumping her off the bed. She knows there'll be food to scavenge soon. "It's far easier to be a cat, cat," I tell her.

I grab my phone. No text from Kevin. 10:01 a.m. Assembly's nearly over and I need to book it to school. But I still don't feel quite human yet and it's not like I can come stumbling in halfway through third period anyway. And besides, at least I'm not stuck in a stuffy auditorium.

I check the OHS feed, where most of my class is grumbling about school, snow, and Mondays, and send off a fake gleeful message. No day like a snow day. Or morning. Whatever.

Kevin's going to give me an earful when he discovers I slept through two alarms, and I can't blame him. He'll be *right*. I worked too hard to get stay on the team to slip up now.

But I'll be there by fourth period, and I'll figure out what to do with Kev then. Perhaps I should just follow Coach's tactics. A good offense is the best defense. Maybe…maybe I should take the first step. Officially ask him out. Kev and I, we're too close for comfort and maybe that's what makes us good together. Comfort is easy. He'd never want to settle. Neither would I. And he knows me in a way that no one else does. Maybe that's a good thing.

I turn on the raggedy oven to heat up the pizza and grab my phone again to set the timer and scroll through sports news websites. 10:05 a.m. At school, the doors of the auditorium will open. Maybe Kev will be on the lookout for me before he heads to his AP Lit class. I open the OHS feed again and slide into his messages:

Rough night. Late morning. I'll explain. See you at fourth?

I smile, hesitantly. Maybe I'll ask him to prom today.

What inspired you to write *This Is Where It Ends*?

Several high-profile school shootings, and a deep long-ing to understand not only the situation, but the human aspect of it. I wanted to understand the *stories* of a school shooting. And *This Is Where It Ends* allowed me to create and explore those stories.

What kind of research did you do to write this book?

A lot of it. For every hour I spent writing, I spent another (at least) researching. I read firsthand accounts of shootings, I listened to 911 calls, I plowed through hundreds of pages of investigative reports, I talked to people, I kept up with news and social media feeds as active shooter situations emerged, I familiarized myself with the psychology of being held at gunpoint. As much as possible, I immersed myself in what we know about school shootings (which is both a lot and not much at all). And I tried to translate that to the book.

At the same time, of course, *This Is Where It Ends* is fic-tion. The story isn't about the technicalities of a shooting;

it's about four teens in a harrowing situation whose world is being turned upside down. So I allowed for that, too, in the way the story unfolded. But I wanted to ensure that any poetic license remained respectful to real life.

What was your writing process like? With four different narrators in *This Is Where It Ends*, how did you keep track of the different voices and timeline?

I'm a plotter at heart, and while plotting this story, I created a massive spreadsheet that tracked, minute by minute, what happened to each of the main characters, as well as the shooter and several other prominent players. It allowed me to keep track of the various arcs of the story, as well as the way different scenes influenced each other. From there, I wrote the story four times, from each of the four different perspectives, to keep the voices distinct. Only then did I start bringing it all together.

Writing like that, with a detailed outline and detailed character profiles, gives me the shape of the story before I start filling it in. It helps me figure out where the important beats are, how to build to the climaxes. I love forming a story like that.

Did the concept or characters come to you first?

In this case, the concept came first, but it was quickly followed by the characters. Once I started wondering

303

about this concept, about these stories, the four main characters found me. Of course, I still had to get to know them through the writing process, but doing so—figuring out their quirks and personalities—was so much fun.

Do you have a favorite character from the novel?

This is such a cruel question, because I spent so much time with each of the characters and I grew so close to them. But if I had to choose, I wouldn't go for one of the four main characters. I would have to say Fareed, who happens to be outside the auditorium when the shooting starts and drops everything because his best friend's sister is in danger. He understands what needs to be done to help a friend in need and does it, no matter the cost.

How did you decide to weave in the text, tweets, and blog posts?

The texts, tweets, and blog posts weren't a part of the first draft of the story. I wanted the main characters to be fairly isolated, and it simply never occurred to me that they'd have cell phones. (I know, I know.) Once my agent very helpfully pointed that out to me, though, I realized what a chance it was. Because of course, nothing of what's happening at Opportunity High School happens in isolation. The world is watching. The students are part of a larger community. And being able to broaden the scope and include those reactions, for better *and* for worse, has been an invaluable addition to the story.

What was the hardest part about writing *This Is Where It Ends*? The most rewarding?

This Is Where It Ends was a very emotional book to work on, both in terms of research and in terms of writing. And occasionally, that would get to be too much. I went on quite a few walks to clear my head. I got lost in video games. I had a number of rituals that helped me deal with the emotion of the book. But in the end, seeing it all come together and seeing the story turn from this collection of scenes and characters to the book I *hoped* to write was entirely rewarding.

What would you like readers to take away from the novel?

Hope. *This Is Where It Ends* is no easy story. Autumn, Claire, Sylv, and Tomás face what may well be every student's worst nightmare. A situation where nothing is safe and survival seems impossible. But it's not a bleak story. There's anger, but there's also friendship. Revenge, but also love. There's family. There's sacrifice. And ultimately, there's the belief that even when the world seems to have stopped turning, when everything has fallen apart, the darkness is never absolute. There is *always* hope.

Has your perception of the book changed since it was published?

I keep hoping the novel will become less relevant. It hasn't so far, and that makes it a very bittersweet book to talk about. I'm proud of it, absolutely. I'm so grateful to all the teachers and librarians who use the book to have difficult conversations with readers, and seeing how it's inspired that dialogue is an honor, quite honestly. But I wish it were less relevant.

You are a native Dutch speaker, yet you wrote *This Is Where It Ends* in English. Have you always written fiction in English? When did you start, and what encouraged you to do so?

I started out writing in Dutch, and I did so all through my teen years. I switched to English in college, because that was when I started traveling. I spent a lot of time in the UK and Ireland, in particular, and made friends from all over the world. Most of them, understandably, didn't speak Dutch, but they were curious about my writing and encouraged me to write something they could read. Writing in English felt entirely natural to me, and once I started, I didn't look back.

Your English novels have been translated into Dutch. Have you read those translations? What was that experience like?

I have read the translations! I got to read along while my Dutch translator worked on the book, and it was the wildest experience. She did a fantastic job. But what made it so magical for me is that, upon reading the full books, I could recognize my own style. There was a clear line, for me at least, from when I still wrote in Dutch to seeing these translations, and that was more than I ever expected.

What is the question you are most asked by readers?

Where I get my inspiration, and what inspired this book, in particular. Obviously, I've already answered the latter, so let me also give you a definitive answer to the former: Everywhere. The world. People. History. Dreams. Other stories. I don't want for inspiration, thankfully.

What is a question you wish readers would ask?

There isn't much I haven't been asked yet, I don't think! But I love it when readers talk to me about what the story meant to them and how they connected with it. I love it when they ask me about the meaning of the story. I love it when they ask me questions I have to think about, because their interpretation sheds a new light on the story, or it focuses on an aspect I hadn't previously thought about.

You talk about the importance books had for you as you were growing up. How has that experience influenced the novels you write?

I read a lot growing up. I easily read hundreds of books a year, and I must've read thousands in total. I read everything. Comics, books, food packaging. I read epic fantasy, literary fiction, sci-fi, myths, legends, thrillers, realism. I read *everything*. Stories gave me entire worlds to get lost in and explore. How has that influenced my own writing? In countless ways and then some. I write for a love of stories. I write to hopefully offer readers that same experience.

At the same time, though, I never found *myself* in stories. Disabled, queer, nonbinary characters were rarely—if ever—the heroes in the books I read growing up. We were tragedy or villains at best. And that felt entirely lonely at times. It took me too long to realize that everyone deserves to be a hero. Stories are for all of us. And stories should remind us that we're not alone. So that is also why I write.

Do you have a favorite book? What makes that book special to you?

Tonke Dragt's *The Letter for the King* is the book that made me a writer. It's a wonderful, adventurous story of a teen boy who wants to become a knight, and I fell deeply in love with it. I was about ten when I first read it. I finished the book, flipped it over, and started again. Then I read the sequel—at least twice. And I decided there and then I wanted to be a writer. I wanted to tell stories like in that book, because it was the first time I'd been completely transported to different worlds.

You talk a lot with teens when you are on tour and through Skype visits with schools and libraries. What is your favorite part about talking about your books with teens?

My books are for teens, first and foremost. So teen feedback is one of my favorite things. I love it when teen readers tell me everything they loved—and sometimes in the same breath, hated—about my books. I love how intensely teens read. I love the art they make. I love the connection they have with the book. I love it when they tell me about their passions and their own writing dreams and plans. Teens are wonderful!

What advice would you give someone who wants to write?

Find your own voice. Tell the story you wish to read. Tell the story you're most passionate about. Write your heart. Write your truth.

If you could share one piece of advice to your teen self,

what would it be?

Keep writing. Just keep writing.

What are seven words you would use to describe your books?

Seven words, right?

All my books will break your heart.

....

Do you have a favorite food or cuisine? Least favorite food?

I love food so much. I love cooking food. I love eating food. And I haven't found anything I absolutely didn't like yet. I could live on various types of bread and soups for months, but I also love discovering new cuisines.

Where is your favorite place to write?

At home, at my desk. Though I love to write on trains and in coffee shops too. But there's something about having all my familiar books around me that is very inspiring.

Pen and paper or typing on computer?

Both. I love pen and paper for plotting and for working through problems, but when the writing is smooth, I love typing.

Would you rather be launched into space or explore the greatest depths of the sea?

Uh, neither? Unless I can be launched into space in a TARDIS or on the USS *Enterprise*. In that case, space, for sure!

What is your superpower? (We know you have lots!)

I'm very good at stealthily observing people and then writing them into books.

If you could have any other superpower, what would it be?

Oh, flight, for sure. I'd love to be able to fly.

Favorite animal?

Falcons! They're so cool.

Favorite movie? TV Show?

Favorite movie is easy: *A Knight's Tale*. For favorite TV show, that's a toss-up between *Doctor Who* and *Star Trek*.

Where is your favorite place you've traveled? Where would you most like to travel?

I loved backpacking around Ireland a few years ago, and I want to go back someday soon. I also love spending time in Edinburgh. As for places I still want to go—I'd love to go to Japan one day!

Do you like to listen to music while you write? What is your karaoke song?

I do listen to music while I write. I have playlists for my books, and I also love instrumental music (whether it's classical music or movie soundtracks or game soundtracks).

My karaoke song? Queen's "Princes of the Universe."

PLAYLIST

"Say Something" | A Great Big World

"Read All About It (Part III)" | Emeli Sandé

"Tam Lin (Child 39)" | Anaïs Mitchell and Jefferson Hamer

"We Don't Eat" | James Vincent McMorrow

"Royals" | Lorde

"Opportunity" | Pete Murray

"Anthem of Our Dying Day" | Story of the Year

"Safe & Sound" | Taylor Swift feat. The Civil Wars

"How to Save a Life" | The Fray

"Utopia" | Within Temptation feat. Chris Jones

ACKNOWLEDGMENTS

My world is richer for the stories it holds, and my life for the community those stories have brought me. Thank you to the authors whose books taught me so much about what it means to be human. To the writers who shared their journeys, manuscripts, and endless support with me. To the readers whose boundless love makes it all worthwhile. And especially:

To Dahlia Adler, Fox Benwell, Corinne Duyvis, and Hannah Weyh. *This Is Where It Ends* would not exist without you. Thank you for friendship, support, insight, excitement, adventures, chats, guest rooms, heart, and inspiration. You make my world a better place.

To my agent, Jennifer Udden, who is the fiercest book champion anyone can wish for. I'd say I'm sorry for making you cry on the subway, but that's really not true. Thank you for believing in me. I'm so happy to have you—and everyone at DMLA—in my corner.

To my editor, Annette Pollert-Morgan, who loves these characters as much as I do and sees right to the heart of the stories I want to tell. Working with you is nothing short of a dream come true. Thank you for your understanding and for pushing me to become a better writer.

(Stroopwafels forever for both of you!)

It's a pleasure and a privilege to be a part of the Sourcebooks family. Thank you to everyone who has made me feel so very welcome. Dominique Raccah and Todd Stocke for their passion and support. Sarah Cardillo, Kelly Lawler, Nicole Komasinski, Isaiah Johnson, and Elizabeth Boyer for their care in the creation of this book. Heather Moore, Beth Oleniczak, and Alex Yeadon, for their creativity, enthusiasm, and general awesomeness. Chris Bauerle, Valerie Pierce, Helen Scott, Sean Murray, Heidi Weiland, and Sara Hartman-Seeskin for their help in bringing this book to the world. And everyone I had the pleasure to interact with or meet.

Along the way, there have been many people who helped me shape this book, and their generosity is humbling. I am so grateful to Hay Farris, Caroline Richmond, and Cindy Rodriguez, who fielded questions on a myriad of topics, and especially so to Alex Brown, who graciously shared relevant experience with the trauma of shootings. What I did right was because of them; any mistakes I made are squarely on me.

Francesca Zappia, Brenda Drake, Erica Chapman, Darci Cole, Jaye Robin Brown, Natalie Blitt, and Jen Malone all read versions of this story and offered invaluable feedback. Thank you for your grace and your honesty.

Just as invaluable was and is the support of amazing writer friends, Katherine Locke, Rebecca Coffindaffer, Maggie Hall, and Gina Ciocca. Thank you adventures in New York / Edinburgh / Paris / Atlanta, for cheering up so many days, for more than I can say.

It's an honor to be on this journey and to share it with so many talented people. I wish I could name each and every one of you. Thank you so much for being here.

A special shout-out to #TeamCupidsLC, for rallying around this story, to the Sweet Sixteens, for our debut year to come, and to Alex Lidell, who took me on the New Jersey road trip where the idea of *This Is Where It Ends* originated.

Last but certainly not least, all of this would be meaningless if it wasn't for the support of my closest friends and family, who have been with me from the start. To Lotte, Lian, Hilda, and Rachael. To my sisters, my nephew, and my mother. This one is for you, with love.